J.H. CURRY

NORMAL

COLLECTION

Hula Twist Press

Published by:

Hula Twist Press

http://jhula02.wordpress.com

A special thanks goes out to the abnormal adolescents that helped me with the cover of this book: Alexandria, Evonna, Kalyna, Izaak and John.

Making the cover for *Normal Collection* was fun and effortless. It is comforting to know that all of you are as twisted as I am. I am speechless. You have now idea how relieved I am that the rotten apple(s) doesn't fall far from the tree.

You make me proud and bring a tear to my eye.

Contents

Normal

Collection

Dear Reader,

Within this *Normal Collection* of short stories and poetry, you, my fine reader, will find darkness. You will find distrust. You will find death. You will find the disturbed.

You will be disturbed.

You, my dear reader, will, upon finishing this collection of work, think differently about others. You will wonder how others think, how others feel, and how others see; and more importantly, when you are through with this book, you will question your *own* sanity. Something that I, myself must do, on a daily basis.

Within *Normal Collection* is the deranged appendage of my first psychological horror novel, *Brothers Huxten*. This work in its entirety is *not* the sequel to my first novel, mind you, but the sequel *is* within. I know that many of you, my precious readers, have been waiting for it. So, here it is. It is in here. The story, *Damon Samuel Higgins*, begins where *Brothers Huxten* left off--a tale of fate of the young newlyweds Jon and Maggie Higgins. It will be the first story you read when you finish this introduction.

You are welcome.

And, my darker and unbalanced poetic works are in here too, the twisted siblings of my first collection of poems that can be found in, *Life's Traveled Roads: A Poetry Chapbook*. So, do connect the poems in *Normal Collection* to my chapbook, a book that is filled with deep and thoughtful poems--pure raw emotion--if you so desire. They are just beautiful.

Now, please, do set some time aside for yourself. Make a cup of coffee, or a cup of tea, or pour a glass of wine--whatever *you* might consume--to help you to relax after a long day, and read my fine work.

I promise you, you will not be disappointed.

Sincerely,
J.H.

Damon Samuel Higgins
1979

The late summer evening couldn't have been more perfect for such a wonderful young couple. Everyone knew that Maggie and Jon had the perfect life waiting out there for them to take hold of...

But--what everyone didn't know--a force was growing. An evil, malevolent being--growing and breathing at that very moment--listening to the laughter of the guests at the wedding reception; listening to the music rolling off of the canvas walls and ceiling of the white tent. Listening. Breathing. Growing.

It was just a tiny little thing. Mommy and Daddy didn't even know that he existed, yet, but they would find out soon enough--and their world as they knew it would be turned upside down forever.

For now, though, Jon and Maggie Higgins were celebrating their union as husband and wife-- celebrating their great new life together.

--Brothers Huxten--

Chapter 1

The honeymoon in the Caribbean was two weeks of bliss for Jon and Maggie. Enjoying the warm air, the solitude, and the water was the perfect way to spend time as Mr. and Mrs. Jon Higgins. A wonderful week of making love in the suite, followed by a week out on the water and in the sand, ended with Maggie's announcement of her pregnancy. Both Jon and Maggie were elated. The tragic events leading up to their marriage were almost completely wiped away. The attack--the rape--all vanished with this one blessing. They flew home to New York and the word quickly spread to the Higgins's friends and family.

***

Maggie's pregnancy was proof that their union was steadfast. Nine months of blissful happiness flew by. They bought a small three-bedroom house outside of town, and spent the entire winter remodeling it until it was finished and perfect. The favorite part of the remodeling for the both of them had been the baby's room. Jon and Maggie chose yellow for the walls with white trim, and Maggie painted a jungle scene on the wall behind the crib.

Maggie was a week overdue, and following through with her doctor's suggestion, she continued doing her regular household chores with hope that she would go into labor. One afternoon, while hanging the white lace curtains in the baby's room, she felt a warm trickle run down her right leg. When she stepped off of the footstool to investigate, she felt a deep pop within her body, and more liquid gushed out, soaking up her soft slippers. For a moment she was amused, and with a laugh, she thought that she must have wet her pants. But, when a cramp quickly caught in her abdomen, she instantly knew that it wasn't urine--her water broke. The baby was coming.

She called her husband into the room and the look in her eyes was all he needed to see that the time had come to go to the hospital.

"Ready?" He asked.

"Ready." Maggie said. Tears sprang from her eyes. "I can't believe that the day is finally here," she said, wiping her eyes with the curtain she was holding. She burst into laughter when she realized what she was using to wipe them.

"Jon, grab the bag next to the crib there...and...I think that we should get going." Another cramp seized her abdomen and she caught her breath. "Yes, we really have to go."

"Okay. Let's get in the car."

The drive there turned from one of excitement to pure horror for the young couple. Maggie's labor intensified to the point where she was uncontrollably screaming out in pain.

Chapter 2

He was a big baby. Breech birth.

He was a little monster of pink, plump flesh. Thirteen pounds and twenty-three inches long. Maggie had mere moments to look at him, to hold him, and then, with a growing look of fear in her eyes said, "Take him away from me. He's different and I don't want to touch him."

Jon took the baby in his arms. He looked down at his son's face and saw something missing in there that he couldn't quite put his finger on.

Her labor had been terrible. Twenty-four hours of strenuous work and no painkillers had left Maggie exhausted. She grew weaker by the second, and her breathing became increasingly shallow while her uterus was painstakingly being replaced back inside of her body; the doctor could not control her excessive bleeding. The poor woman could barely look up at her husband.

"Jon," Maggie called to her husband, "my love." Quickly, without looking, Jon handed their son to the nearest nurse and then looked in his lovely young bride's eyes. She was slipping away from him. Against her doctor's advice, Jon gently lay down next to her on the blood-soaked bed, wrapping her in his arms.

"Maggie, don't leave me, my baby, *please*, I can't live without you. Fight. Don't go," he whispered into her ear, "I need you." All of the others in the room faded into the background. To Jon, all that mattered, at that moment, was just he and his wife.

"Jon," she whispered once more, "be careful."

"What?" He asked. "Don't talk. Just fight. Fight for us. Breathe. Just breathe. Don't leave me. I love you. Don't go."

"I love you," her cool lips touched his. Tears fell from Maggie's closed eyes just as the surgeon walked in. "Maggie!" Jon screamed out her name, shaking her, "Wake up! Please, wake up." Two nurses took to the task of peeling him away from her and whisked him out of the room, placing him in the hall.

The infant was rushed out of the room as well, and taken to the nursery. Stunned, Jon stood outside of the delivery room while the nurse walked passed him with the baby, but he could not bear to look at him at that time, because his wife's defeated body was all that he could think about. Nine months. *Nine months* was all that they had together after their memorable wedding. Nine months of anxiously awaiting the arrival of their child--getting the house ready--adding personal touches to it. Painting the cozy little room at the end of the hall that warm yellow. Buying the crib, the clothes, and the tiny blankets. Everything was waiting for them back at their tidy cape.

These thoughts and countless others poured into Jon's mind while he stood there motionless in the hallway. During her whole pregnancy, Maggie had a recurring nightmare of dying during childbirth. She would awake in the middle of the night screaming in terror--shaking--calling out to Jon. And, on those nights to calm her, he would simply say to her that it was just the jitters, and that she should forget about it and go back to sleep; he should have taken her a little more seriously. Maybe, he should have listened to her. Maybe, if, he hadn't jokingly shrugged off her nightmare and had in fact listened to what she was worried about, maybe, then just maybe, she would be here to enjoy what was supposed to be one of the greatest days of their lives. It wasn't supposed to be this way.

What happened? Why them? What did they do wrong? Jon did not know. They had suffered enough, hadn't they? Their escape from certain death almost a year ago, from that man, that *psycho*, that they had the misfortune of meeting last summer. The rape. Their miraculous recovery from the experience. Terrifying. They did not deserve what was happening now. *Maggie* did not deserve this! Jon couldn't believe any of it. His wife, his soul mate, still in the delivery room, gone. Their baby, their little boy, just down the hall in the nursery--was a person he cared not to see.

Chapter 3

Several nurses and the surgeon emerged from the delivery room with Maggie and rushed down the hall to the elevator. The sheet covering her was soaked with blood--such a horrible sight. The sound of the wheels of the hospital bed reached Jon's ears. To him, the sound was grating--it was the loudest, most painful sound that he had ever heard in his entire life. Squeak. Squeak. Squeak. Squeak. Squeak. Squeak. Squeak. Squeak. Squeak. Damn, how long *was* the hall? Jon couldn't help but feel that the squeaking, *mocking* wheels, were taking his wife away from him.

How could this have happened? What happened? Why? These thoughts were turning over and over on an endless loop inside Jon's head while he made his way to the visitor's area--collapsing on the couch. He gasped when he heard the elevator door open and close at the end of the hall. He was heartbroken.

Seconds later, Jon heard the baby, *his baby*, crying in the nursery. He knew that it was his. *Just knew it.* The sound was so strange. Otherworldly. So full of life. So strong. But, yet, it was quite different from a regular baby's cry in Jon's mind. Deeper, *darker*, louder. He had no desire to see him. To see *it*. He couldn't help but think that *kid*, that *thing* was the reason for Maggie's suffering, the reason for his suffering.

Damon. Damon was what Maggie had wanted to name their child. Damon Samuel Higgins. As soon as she found herself pregnant, that was the name that had popped into her mind. "No matter if it is a boy or a girl," Maggie had said one night while they were in bed together, "no matter what, I want our child to be named Damon. To me, it sounds perfect." Jon didn't really care much for the name himself. It struck an odd chord within his brain. The name itself had a sickening quality. Damon. Damon. Like, like, *Damn son*. The name *Damon* just did not sit with him well. But, Maggie absolutely loved it, and that was the name that stuck.

Now, Damon, the mammoth baby down the hall, was for Jon's and Jon's alone to take home. Maggie would not be there. His head hurt--he couldn't think that far ahead. What was he to do--ask his mom and his dad to take the child from him? His in-laws? *Oh God!* How was he to break the news to everyone?

Everyone will be devastated--they will all want to know what had happened during the delivery. They will all ask what went wrong, and, why wouldn't they? And, his in-laws, *his in-laws*, the two with the money, they will march right down to the hospital themselves, and demand an explanation as to why their beloved daughter was not taken care of properly.

Minutes had passed while Jon sat in that room. Maggie was gone to who knows where. Jon overheard the surgeon barking orders so quickly that the delivery room was cleared in a matter of seconds. The gorgeous woman that he had married was now defeated. The woman that was so young and amazing was now gone. Her beautiful blue eyes were now closed. Vacant. Empty. Cold. Her blonde, curly hair--will no longer soak up the sunlight. Her laugh--her *laugh*! That soft, sexy laugh--was to never be heard by his ears again. She was gone. *Gone!* Jon placed his head in his hands and sobbed. His wavy brown hair, all disheveled, hung over his forehead.

A nurse at the nurses' station heard him, and decided to come in and offer some comfort to him as best as she could. She had just arrived for her shift and had heard of the tough delivery.

"Mr. Higgins," she said, she sat down beside him, putting her hand on his shoulder; "I was wondering…do you need anything? Do you want me to run down to the cafeteria to get you something to eat? You need to keep up your strength."

Jon looked up at her. His eyes were blood shot and his eyelids were puffy; his face was soaked with his sweat and tears. He quickly wiped his hand across his eyes and tried to be as pleasant as he could.

"No. Thanks for offering. I'm...I'm just not that very hungry right now."

"Are you sure?" She asked. "It wouldn't take but only a minute."

"No," Jon looked at the name tag on her left breast pocket, "I'm fine. Thanks, Ruthie, I just want to be left alone."

"Well, if you should change your mind, I will be in the nursery tending to the infants. Some of them are my patients tonight, and I do believe that your little boy is one of them. So, if you are up to it, you should come on in there and help me feed him." Smiling, Ruthie patted Jon's shoulder, got up, and left the waiting room.

Chapter 4

While Jon was sitting there in the dark, he heard his little boy cry out once more. For Maggie's sake, Jon pushed himself up off of the couch and made his way out of the room and down the hall to the nursery. He stopped in front of the large window and looked in-- there was Damon. The biggest baby in the room. You couldn't miss him. He was huge. Nurse Ruthie was approaching his crib with a bottle in her hand. Briefly, she glanced up, saw that Jon was looking through the window, and smiled. As Jon looked on, she set the bottle of formula down on a stand that was by a rocking chair, and then she approached Damon's crib. Swiftly and expertly, Nurse Ruthie picked up the wriggling wrapped bundle, and then proceeded to sit down in the rocking chair to feed him.

Jon noticed that Damon took to the bottle without a problem; he almost completely guzzled down the formula within seconds. Jon could tell that Ruthie was very surprised that the baby had done so, too, just as he was. She was quite accustomed to infants fussing about the nipple, and sometimes not even taking to it at first, so this was very unusual. While Nurse Ruthie studied Damon's pudgy face as he sucked down the remaining drops of the formula, she suddenly became aware, and then quite uncomfortable when she realized, that the little boy was studying her, too.

As Ruthie rocked Damon, and Jon looked on through the glass, out of nowhere, what sounded like a deep muffled growl had risen in the room. With a perplexed look on her face, Nurse Ruthie looked about the room, thinking that perhaps the heat had kicked on; but she shook her head, for she instantly knew that *that* wasn't the noise, because, she could differentiate *that* sound already humming along the tiled floor. So again she focused her attention on the sound, and then grew alarmed upon realizing that the growling was coming from the *baby* she was holding.

Without warning--projectile vomit shot from Damon and hit Ruthie directly in the face--she instantly wiped her face with the sleeve of her sweater. As soon as she had done this, however, Damon went and did it again. This time the vomit was so sticky that she panicked when she couldn't get it out of her eyes. Ruthie then called out for help and two nurses came running in; one of them took Damon out of her hands and placed him back in the crib while the other nurse assisted Ruthie. Jon ran in to see if he could be of any help, as well.

When Ruthie's two companions were finally able to force her hands down from her face, they, too, cried out in surprise--Ruthie's face was raw and inflamed. The flesh around her eyes had sagged and blood was trickling down her cheeks and onto her sweater. To Jon, it looked like acid had been splashed on her. As calmly as they could, the two nurses directed their injured friend out of the nursery to have her wounds attended to. As they rushed passed him, Jon heard one of them mumble to the other that the formula that Ruthie had fed Damon must have had a chemical reaction of some sort, and luckily, she didn't think that Ruthie was blinded by the event.

Jon walked over to Damon's crib and looked down at him. Damon was sound asleep and snoring loudly. Jon couldn't help but despise the child. The thing was only hours old and it was already causing problems for anyone that had gotten near it. Jon's mind was racing. What was he to *do*? Should he put this kid up for adoption? *He* certainly didn't want it. And-- where was Maggie? What were they doing to her? He turned and walked out of the nursery and back to the waiting room.

As he sat back down on the couch in the waiting room and was leaning back to rest his eyes, he heard someone clear their throat. Upon opening them to see who it was, his heart skipped a beat; the surgeon from the delivery room was standing in the doorway.

"Mr. Higgins, I am so sorry to have rushed out of the delivery room the way that I did, but you know that I didn't have a choice in the matter, there wasn't a moment to spare. You understand that, right?"

Jon nodded, and the surgeon walked over and sat down next to him to deliver the rest of news. Jon felt his heart quicken in his chest and a bead of sweat trickled down his back. He braced himself.

"Maggie is stable. She needed emergency surgery, she needed several blood transfusions, but she is now in the recovery room and is resting comfortably. It will take her several weeks, but I feel that Maggie will be well in no time and she will recover completely."

Jon blinked. He couldn't have heard the surgeon correctly. Maggie couldn't be alive? She was barely breathing after Damon was born. She was in labor for hours and had lost so much blood.

The surgeon saw the look of disbelief on Jon's face, so he put his hand on Jon's shoulder and smiled, "Yes, Jon, yes, you heard me correctly, Maggie is good. Maggie is alive. She is one tough little lady. Pretty soon, the two of you will be back home with that precious baby boy of yours. I am so happy for all of you."

Jon began to cry, "Oh my God, my God, I can't believe it! Thank you. Thank you for saving her. Thank you." Jon couldn't help himself--he hugged the surgeon--the surgeon didn't resist, and hugged him back, for he was just as relieved as Jon was; Maggie had been the toughest patient that he had ever come across in his entire career. During the surgery, he himself thought that she wasn't going to make it.

Minutes later, before leaving the waiting room, the surgeon mentioned to Jon that he could see Maggie in an hour or so but very briefly, and added that with proper rest and if everything went smoothly, Maggie would be able to go home in several weeks. He bid Jon a goodnight and walked away.

***

Chapter 5

The following weeks went by slowly. Jon did his best to take care of Damon on his own at home. Reluctantly, though, he had to rely heavily upon his mother for her assistance, and she was with him as much as she could be. At first, Mrs. Higgins was very supportive and quite thrilled to lend a hand. Damon was her first grandchild, and she loved being near him and cherished every moment that she spent with him. But, by the end of the third week, Jon's mother was becoming more and more nervous and uncomfortable around her grandson. She tried her best to hide her discomfort from Jon because she didn't want to burden him with her problems. The last few weeks had been very difficult for him; he had taken a leave of absence from his job to be able to split his time between caring for Damon, and visiting Maggie at the hospital. Mrs. Higgins knew that the situation was tough. But, at times, her uneasiness got the better of her and she would mention in passing that Damon was surely a different baby--one that she had never known before. Jon would make the attempt to get out of his mother just what she meant when she made her comments. He was secretly wishing to see if she saw Damon for the *thing* that *he* saw him as, but she would always shrug off his questioning and change the subject.

Eventually, Mrs. Higgins noticed that caring for Damon was starting to take its toll on her health and well-being. She couldn't quite explain what was happening to her, but spending her days and some of her nights with him while Jon was away at the hospital had left her exhausted. At first, she blamed it on simple fatigue. She reminded herself that she was in fact older, after all, and that she wasn't some twenty-something spring chicken taking care of a baby, and her exhaustion was simply due to her age. But as the days wore on, Mrs. Higgins realized that on some mornings, (mornings after the terrible recurring nightmare she would have of three-week-old Damon climbing out of his crib, crawling after her at a freakishly unnatural pace, catching her, knocking her down, and eating her alive) she had difficulty getting out of bed. And at one point, when she realized that her clothes were starting to get very loose on her, she went and weighed herself, and was alarmed to see that she had lost twenty-five pounds.

To make matters worse, one afternoon, while eating a sandwich during lunch, Mrs. Higgins felt two back molars crack and split, and then simply fall onto her tongue. Frightened, she rushed to the bathroom to take out the pieces of her teeth, and as she pulled back her long hair to spit the blood out of her mouth, she gasped when hundreds of strands fell out in her hands. Afterward, when she had gotten herself cleaned up and wiped the blood from her lips, she caught sight of her reflection in the mirror and cried out in shock--she looked nothing like her former self. Her hair was very thin, she had more gray strands in it than she did only weeks ago, her eyes were sunken in and they had dark circles underneath them. Sadly, Mrs. Higgins could not help but cry, when she realized that she looked like a wasted woman, barely alive--a skull with loose skin.

On the morning of the day that Damon was exactly a month old, Jon had left to go and pick up Maggie from the hospital to bring her home. Mrs. Higgins was ashamed to admit it, but she couldn't help but be relieved. She knew that Jon and Maggie would still need her help, but she couldn't wait for the burden to lessen for her. She was finally being honest with herself and accepted the fact that she simply didn't have it in her to take care of Damon much longer, and that he needed his parents more than he needed her. She would never outright admit it to anyone, especially Jon and Maggie, but she truly felt that her declining health was the direct result of Damon, and that Damon, however possible, was slowly killing her--and enjoying it. She only needed to look in his eyes to see that this was true.

Finally, Mrs. Higgins realized, that as much as she loved Damon Samuel, she needed to distance herself from him, or she would surely be dead in just a few months.

***

Chapter 6

Jon parked the car in front of the entrance at the hospital. Maggie knew that he would be up to get her in a few minutes, so for a moment, he just sat there and rested his head back on the headrest of his seat. His mind was racing. His mother's deteriorating health did not go unnoticed. He saw how she was withering away at an alarming pace, and he knew that getting Maggie home would be good for all of them. Mom, being the tough woman that she was, was putting on a brave face, but he knew that she was quite relieved, and rightly so, that Maggie would be home shortly.

Jon's mother would never admit it to him, or to Dad, or to anyone--that caring for Damon Samuel was slowly killing her--but Jon knew. He knew that Damon was *literally* sucking the life right out of her--and him. Luckily, but sadly speaking, Mom was so preoccupied with Damon's demands so much, that she failed to see that Jon's energy was draining too--and honestly--he was quite relieved for this one small blessing. His mother had her own health to worry about, and she didn't need to be worrying about him. He actually wanted her out of his house so that she could get the chance to recover and to get healthy again.

Jon saw early on what Damon was capable of, he had tried to kill his *own* mother during his birth, which was also why he had kept his in-laws and his father away from Damon, as well. It was easy enough-- all of them worked and kept busy hours--but when they did stop by the house to visit, Jon couldn't help but notice how they all complained of fatigue, and would even be physically ill several days afterward. He also kept tabs on Nurse Ruthie to make sure that she was recovering as much as she could. The last he knew, Ruthie had taken a paid leave of absence to heal and to have surgery on her face, and the results had been great. The hospital, Ruthie's family, and the company that made the infant formula were in legal negotiations, and a settlement was being reached. Jon was happy for Nurse Ruthie, was happy to hear that she would make a complete recovery--but *he* knew what really happened. He just *knew*. He was *convinced*. It was Jon's firm belief that the closer an individual got to Damon, that the more someone held him, the more someone cared for him, and the deeper someone loved him--that person would eventually be destroyed by him.

Damon was little, now, but Jon couldn't help think of and worry about what Damon would be capable of in a few more weeks. In a few more months--in years! Jon didn't know *how* Damon was doing it. He certainly didn't know *why* he was doing it, but--he *was*. And, Jon just knew that deep down--there would be no stopping him.

The last month had been brutal, and Jon knew that this last month had just been a trial run for Damon. Damon was testing the waters, so to speak. Damon was trying to get a feel for how much damage he could do just as an infant, or, rather, how much damage he could accomplish in his *infant form*.

There was no denying it--this past month had been filled with ill-health for Jon and his family. This past month had been filled with sleepless nights. This past month was filled with Jon waking to find Damon sitting on his chest--sucking and licking at his skin; it was a month full of a recurring nightmare, (a nightmare of Damon overpowering and killing everyone that Jon loved, everyone that Jon held close). A nightmare, Jon was convinced, would one day become reality. And, Jon couldn't help but notice, couldn't help but connect Damon and all of these events, to those of someone that he and Maggie had befriended at a bar, and then had the misfortune to trust. A certain someone that he and Maggie had tried desperately to forget about. A malicious and evil man that had lured them into a motel room last summer, and then tied them up. A man--that sucked the blood from Maggie's neck while he raped her--a man that tried to kill them both. A *being*--that tried to eat them. To *destroy* them. The connection couldn't be ignored. It was real.

In all actuality, the traumatic event of last summer didn't really *leave* Jon and Maggie--and it never would. As hard as they tried to ignore it, as hard as they tried to pretend that it didn't happen, it was always there, eating away at them, and it couldn't be denied any longer. It was very much alive and breathing. In fact, it was at home right now, in its crib, slowly killing Grandma--and enjoying it. Damon Samuel Higgins, Damn-son, *It*, *Thing*--whatever *he* was--*it* was--whatever you wanted to call him--was waiting for Mommy and Daddy to come home.

***

Chapter 7

Maggie was emotionally torn. She was happy, but yet, very hesitant to leave the hospital. She missed Jon desperately. He had visited her as much as he could while she was recovering, but it wasn't the same, and so she was thrilled to be leaving. She desperately wanted to be back at home, with Jon, and not stuck in the hospital environment; but, still, she couldn't help but think, couldn't help but *know*, that she was safer in here, in the hospital, than she would be when she got home. Because that *thing* was there--waiting for her.

Jon kept Maggie up to date with what was happening at the house. He told her about his mother, and that he feared for her health. And, Maggie knew that these weren't exaggerated stories, because she could see with her own eyes what Damon was doing to Jon, as well. He looked terrible. The twinkle in his eyes that she loved so much to see was gone. He had lost weight. He looked disheveled and exhausted, and it didn't improve as the weeks went by, it only had gotten worse.

Damon Samuel was supposed to be the glue that kept Jon and Maggie sane. After what had happened to them last summer--what had happened to *her*--had almost killed the both of them, they needed normalcy. She knew that they would be forever scarred by that night, and she thought that having a child would help them heal. She wondered, sometimes, though, if not pressing charges, if not getting to the end of the matter, had caused more harm than good. For months, Maggie felt that by not getting closure, there would always be a part of her soul, and Jon's too, that would forever be blackened by that night. She had felt this way even after their wedding. Even after she had found out that she was pregnant with Damon Samuel.

At the end of that summer, Maggie never expressed her thoughts and concerns to Jon, but she did often wonder about whatever happened to the maniac that tortured them. She wanted to believe that the man was dead--n*eeded* for him to be dead. She wanted to believe that he met a bitter end. Fortunately for her, however, not too long after the incident in the motel room, Maggie had read in the paper, and then saw on the news, that a killing spree occurred in a nearby town--Jordantown--was the name of the place. A small community west of her hometown that saw a summer of murder; and in the end, two brothers--Buddy and Theo Huxten--names that Maggie knew she would never forget, twins, they were, were found dead in some swamp on the family farm. Reports stated that Buddy

Huxten had died of a massive heart attack, and Theo died of a gun shot wound inflicted by his brother; apparently the brothers were caught up in some sort of love triangle that went awry, which resulted in the deaths of at least seven people. Brutal, it was. The attacks on a couple of the victims in Jordantown were quite similar to what Maggie and Jon endured on the night in that motel room. Deep down, Maggie *knew* that it was more than just a coincidence that her traumatic event, and the events that had happened in Jordantown were connected, and, she couldn't let the matter go.

Maggie thought that perhaps one of the twins was her attacker, and the more she kept herself up to date with that tragic news story, the more she had a firm belief that yes, one of those brothers that died in that swamp was in fact hers and Jon's attacker. And, as soon as she knew, deep within her heart, that she was correct in her assumption, she was finally at peace with not pursuing the incident. The oppressing shadow that settled over her and Jon had lifted a little, and she began to grow happy once again.

When Maggie first found out that she was pregnant she was confident that the baby was hers and Jon's. It *needed* to be so, and Maggie knew that was what Jon needed, too. But, when her nightmare began, when she dreamed over and over that the baby would kill her during childbirth, she grew worried, and began to feel that the baby wasn't Jon's after all. Half-halfheartedly, half-jokingly, Maggie even thought to herself that Damon Samuel was not just the son, but also the reincarnate of the man that tortured them last summer.

That recurring nightmare was the worst that she had ever had. It always began the same way: her water would break, the fluid having the distinct odor of stagnant, damp air--it was very foul smelling--like the smell of a dark cellar; then, the baby, always a boy, would come tearing out of her, painfully, brutally, clawing its way out and leaving her torn and bleeding. But, that wasn't the worst part of it. In the dream, Maggie, suffering from the birth, dying, gasping for breath, would, with every ounce of strength she had left in her, pick the baby up in her arms--and scream. The baby would not be a baby after all, rather, it would be the man that attacked her and Jon in the motel room. It would be the balding, foul, jagged-yellow-toothed nasty creature--pure evil pushed out from the depths of *Hell* itself. It was a face that she would never forget. And, before she would wake up, the baby would always turn to look at her, look at her with its dark, soulless eyes, and jump on her face, and start to feast.

The thought of that nightmare still sent shivers down Maggie's spine. She had never given Jon the full details of that dream because she still was hoping for that happy ending. After Damon's actual birth, however, she knew the truth. After nearly dying in real life because of his birth, and after taking one look at him on that day in the delivery room, she knew. When she felt herself fading, when she felt her life slipping away after Damon's birth, she knew. And, *thankfully*, when she awoke in the recovery room and realized that she would live, when she realized that she had been given a second chance to take charge of her fate, she took the time in there to think. She had one good, solid month to plan and to think. Finally, after accepting what she needed to do, she and Jon put their heads together, and that was when they realized that they had had the same thought all along. What they weren't communicating to each other--was being thought about by both. They compared their thoughts and ideas, and agreed that the only happy ending they would be able to have, the only way they would be able to survive, would be a direct result of what they *knew* they had to do.

***

Chapter 8

Jon and Maggie dared tell no one of their plan. They agreed that it was for the best, and as a consequence, they unfortunately had to keep Mrs. Higgins at the house for just a little longer until they were both back home; so as the days passed, and as Maggie grew stronger, they agreed that Jon needed to visit her less frequently to keep his mother as safe as he could. It was a tough decision to make, for they knew that they were gambling with *all* of their lives, but Jon and Maggie agreed that their plan would only succeed, would only work, when Damon felt comfortable and thought that he was the one that was in control.

Maggie and Jon knew that to an outsider, all of this planning to kill an innocent, helpless baby, was a terrible and unimaginable crime--and rightly so--but no one knew Damon Samuel like the two of them did. Damon Samuel Higgins was no innocent, helpless baby. There was no denying it--in just one short month of his life--Damon had destroyed others. He almost blinded a nurse. He tried to kill his mother while being born. He was slowly killing his grandmother and father.

No, Damon Samuel Higgins was *not* normal. He was some sort of demon in disguise--and both Maggie and Jon knew the truth--*Damon Samuel needed to die*.

Jon and Maggie agreed that they would have to kill Damon together, and quickly, and most importantly, make it look like an accident. They thought of the countless ways to kill the child. First, Jon suggested creating a car accident where they'd survive, but Damon wouldn't; but Maggie decided against this because this way wasn't foolproof and a multitude of things could go wrong. Second, they thought of stabbing him to death, but they agreed that they both truly didn't know what Damon was capable of, and he might very easily overpower them in the process.

A third option Jon and Maggie considered, was to abandon him in the house, perhaps even in the cellar, but they soon realized that wouldn't work, because

Damon had excellent survival skills; and for some reason or another, leaving him behind in that way seemed to reassure their belief that it would only fuel his anger toward them, and anyone else that got in his way. So, after days of figuring out how they should do it, they came up with a fourth, and final, solution. Jon and Maggie concluded that there was only one sure way to kill Damon Samuel--sedation and fire.

***

So--on the morning that she was to be discharged from the hospital--Maggie had asked her doctor for a prescription for anxiety medication. She claimed that she was having trouble relaxing, and admitted that she was a bit nervous to be going home to an infant that she hadn't really seen. The doctor had no qualms about doing so and happily agreed, so Maggie had a three-month prescription attached to her discharge papers.

After her release, Jon and Maggie drove to the drugstore to get the prescription, and some milk and groceries, before returning home. While sitting in the store's parking lot, they very carefully crushed the pills into the cartons of milk that they knew only Damon Samuel would be drinking from.

***

Chapter 9

When Jon and Maggie walked into their home late that afternoon, they weren't surprised that an excited reception greeting them upon Maggie's arrival home, wasn't there. There were no flowers, or balloons, or presents, or welcoming banner. The house was dark- -and sad. Mrs. Higgins was sitting in a chair at the kitchen table with big, fat, pink and ugly Damon Samuel on her lap. Maggie couldn't hide her utter shock when she compared the two, and while Jon was putting away the groceries, the pained expression on his face made it clear to Maggie that Mrs. Higgins looked worse than she had when he had left the house that morning. Pretty Mrs. Higgins, always properly dressed and groomed, always eager with a warm and inviting smile, was pretty no more. Whereas Damon grew, and outgrew, all of his baby clothes and could now only fit into adult diapers, Mrs. Higgins shrunk, and was now no more than a bag of bones. Her skin was dry and gray. She was practically bald, with only a few wispy strands remaining on her once full head of thick, beautiful hair. Her mouth was agape, and Maggie could see that she was missing several teeth. The smell of her decaying sickness filled the room. Maggie gagged and couldn't hold back her tears. Damon Samuel, huge and ugly, dwarfed his grandmother.

Turning to look at his parents, Damon pushed off of his grandmother, discarding her like yesterday's trash. Grunting, he then crawled over to his parents, climbing up Maggie's leg like a greedy animal, almost knocking her off of her feet--Jon had to grab her to steady her.

To Maggie, Damon felt at least sixty pounds, huge, for a month old baby, "He's crawling? He's *enormous*."

"He never stops eating. He just doesn't." Mrs. Higgins replied. The effort to speak was making it hard for her to breathe.

Jon walked over to his mother and gently helped her up, "Mom, let me get you in the car to take you home. Dad's waiting. You need to leave here...Dad needs to take care of you, now. He knows that you need to be home with him. And, listen, I don't want you back here again until you are healthy. Do you understand?"

Nodding, Mrs. Higgins looked in her son's eyes, and then together, they laboriously walked toward the front door. Maggie quickly planted a kiss on Mrs. Higgins's sunken cheek as she walked by. There was a look of pure relief upon Mrs. Higgins's face as Jon escorted her out the door.

With much effort, Maggie carried Damon to the living room and sat down on the couch with him. For a fleeting moment, for one hopeful moment, a mother's love tricked her into thinking that Damon's excitement to see her was a baby's love for its mother; but that was a mistake--for as soon as she sat down, he lifted her shirt, tore at her bra until it snapped, and viciously began to nurse at her breast.

His suckling was unbearable. She could *feel* his power. His slurping, tugging and chomping on her with his gums was making her bleed. As she sat there gritting her teeth, careful not to make the slightest noise of discomfort, feeling herself weaken, she reminded herself that she needed to do this. She knew that she had to make Damon comfortable around her and Jon. It was the only way. It *had* to be done. They had discussed it many times in the last couple of days. Their plan was already in motion. They couldn't bail out now. They agreed that they had to be cautious from now on until their plan took hold, or Damon would catch on, and soon be too big and out of their control to be able to do anything.

Chapter 10

Arriving home after taking his mother back to her house that evening, Jon found Maggie in the kitchen making dinner. A part of him so desperately wanted what he was seeing to be true--Maggie bustling about, happy, and Damon on a blue blanket on the floor nearby, playing. But it wasn't reality. He could clearly see Maggie was trying her best to fake the happiness, and when she turned toward him and offered up her best superficial smile, the look in her eyes sold her out-- she was acting. Jon suppressed his outrage when he saw her bloodstained shirt, her sunken cheeks, and the dark circles underneath her eyes. She was already being drained. Damon was definitely moving at a faster pace than he was just that morning.

***

Jon and Maggie sat quietly at the dinner table trying their best to make their small talk convincing in front of Damon. So far, he didn't seem to notice, or care that they were even there. Damon didn't need them at all. When he was done playing, and decided that he was hungry, Damon simply crawled to the refrigerator, opened it up, and grabbed the first carton of milk. Tossing it aside after he was done with it, he then grabbed last night's chicken carcass, dragged it back to his blanket, and gummed it, bones and all.

Watching him eat, Maggie put a smile behind her voice, to mask its trembling, "My little boy...you have quite the appetite! Mommy is so proud of you."

"Yup, that's my boy! He loves his food," Jon said. In response, Damon glanced at his parents and growled, guarding his food like a wild animal. Jon and Maggie got up slowly and then cleared the table-- mindful of the large baby on the floor--they dared not disturb him.

Luckily, the night went by smoothly. All evening, Damon consumed the drugged milk--polishing it off like Jon said he would. However, they both grew uneasy when it appeared that the anxiety medication wasn't working. According to Jon, Damon wasn't slowing down, and he was sticking to his nightly ritual: crawling about the house, grabbing food, milk, and doing whatever pleased him.

Remaining diligent, however, and acting as normal as they could, Jon and Maggie stayed close by and did not keep their distance from Damon so he wouldn't grow suspicious. They watched TV for a while, and then they played a couple of card games, patiently waiting for midnight, when Damon would crawl off to his crib to go to sleep.

When Damon made yet another trip to the kitchen, Jon's heart skipped a beat when he saw him take a little tumble. Finally, the medication was coursing through Damon's system. While Damon was sluggishly slurping and gulping down the remaining milk in the kitchen, struggling to stay upright on the floor while he drank, Maggie quietly got up and went about the house, lighting candles. Having candles in every room wasn't something new and unusual to Damon, and lighting them up didn't seem to alarm him at all. He was too preoccupied with his feeding and sleepiness to watch Maggie, so if he was suspicious of her behavior, it didn't show, and, he seemed not to care.

Damon finished the last drop of milk and slowly crawled away to his nursery. Jon told Maggie that Damon fell asleep relatively quickly, but that they had only a good, solid, two-hour window between midnight and two in the morning before Damon would stir and get up. Maggie followed behind him and watched him hoist himself up into his crib. It was quite unnerving to watch an infant unnaturally propel itself up and then into its bed with supernatural strength, and for Maggie, the eerie glow of the lighted candles didn't help with what she was seeing, either. Despite this, though, her curiosity got the better of her, and Maggie made an attempt to get a little closer to watch Damon settle in, for it would be the first, and last time, that she would see him do this.

When she got to the edge of his crib and bent down to get a good look at him, he snarled and reached up, scratching her chest. Fortunately, she jumped back just in time, and only shallow scratches could be seen. She quickly left the room before she aggravated him any further.

Calmly, Maggie and Jon waited in the living room for about thirty minutes before Maggie tiptoed back to the nursery to see if Damon Samuel was asleep. Seeing that he was, and upon hearing his snoring, she quietly walked over to the dresser where she had placed a candle, grabbed it, and put it on the floor underneath the curtains--ironically--the same curtains that she was holding the day her water broke. Quickly pushing the other candles over, she took one last look at the evil being sleeping in its crib before walking out, closing the door behind her. Afterward, Jon and Maggie went through the house pushing the remaining candles over, and placing others on the floor underneath curtains and on the carpeting.

With only the clothes on their backs--Jon and Maggie Higgins walked out the front door.

***

Chapter 11

The local news reported the fire. According to their statement to the police, Jon and Maggie barely made it out of the house alive. They both had fallen asleep in front of the TV when they smelled smoke and awoke to the house ablaze. Jon stated that he had desperately made every attempt to get to the nursery to rescue Damon, but the house was already thick with smoke, and the fire was so intense that Jon couldn't get close to the room at all.

After the firefighters put out the flames, and it was safe for them to go into what was left of the house, they searched and had found Damon Samuel Higgins's charred remains. Everyone knew that Jon and Maggie were devastated about the death of their infant son, but they all knew that together, the two would get through it, and with time, they would heal and would be able to move on with their lives.

***

Chapter 12

At Jon and Maggie's request, a private funeral was held for their baby boy, and only family members were permitted to attend. It was a simple service at the cemetery in the woods on Maggie's family estate--a closed casket with some flowers.

Afterward--when all of the other family members had left, and when Maggie and Jon surely knew that they were alone in the cemetery, they jumped down into the grave, opened the casket--and proceeded to violently crush Damon's charred remains with their bare hands. The ashes flew everywhere. Jon and Maggie were covered with it. The gray powder was on their clothes, on their skin, in their hair, in their eyes; it went into their nostrils, settled deep within their lungs-- they could even taste its bitterness on the tongue. It made them cough and gag and sneeze, but they couldn't and wouldn't stop until they were finished.

When they were done, they closed the empty casket, climbed out of the gaping hole, and left. Hand in hand, they walked out of the wooded cemetery and down the hill--a cloud of gray dust was left in their wake.

Jon and Maggie Higgins wanted to be certain. The wonderful young couple absolutely, positively, beyond a shadow of a doubt, wanted to make sure--that Damon Samuel Higgins was dead--and dead he was.

Ditch Dweller Devotion

As a child, my mama told me a bedtime story about a ditch.

A deep.
A dark.
A *dangerous*--
one hell of a scary ditch.

A ditch at the edge of the town.

And, she told me, just so that she could scare me, that if I wasn't careful, and that if I wasn't a good little girl, I would fall into it.

And never to be seen or heard from again.

This so-called ditch was deep and dirty.
Its decaying leaves were black and slimy.
A *monster* trudged along in this ditch daily.
Stumbling in the thick sludge.

This ditch was so deep that the feet up above were eye-level.

Colorful shoes walked above the monster's face at his eye-level.

Walking.

Walking.
Busy, walking.
Walking along in their everyday lives.

And sometimes, this monster would get bored, or get
hungry, or maybe even angry, and would reach up,
hoping, hoping--to grab someone with his gnarled hand.

To grab someone with his twisted (*his gorgeous)* his
rough (*his rugged)* gnarled hand.

And eat.

For he was mad, sad, and hungry.

And, sometimes, he would cry out, his (*beautiful*) voice
would *roar* and ring *out,* because sometimes,
sometimes, he wanted attention.

He wanted someone to join him in his endless place,
in his endless, eternal, sad, dark place.

(*And--I was the only one that knew that this was so.*)

But, for the others, no one dared to touch him, though.
For, people were afraid of him--and rightly so.
But, he fascinated *me*--though.

And, I thought about him daily.

As I grew older, and stronger, unfearing, and more daring, I would go looking for this monster and his ditch.

I would search for this beautiful creature,
this amazing, ravishing, *glorious* creature, and his dirty, filthy, dark, dank ditch.

I searched everywhere.

Mama told me to leave him alone.
Mama told me to not go near his home.
For my mama feared that he would eat me so.
But, I wouldn't, and couldn't, listen.

One day I found his ditch and stepped to the edge of it.
I craned my neck to look out, down, and over the edge of it--and there he was!

And oh, what a beautiful, *beautiful* beast he was.

He was big.
He was brawn.
He was hairy.
He was strong.
And he smelled of rot and death!

He was perfect.

He didn't look too friendly, however,
he didn't like people staring.

Which made me love him even more.

And, like always--he thought that I was there like the others that had been before.
He thought that I was there to kick the dirt into his face like others had done before.

To get the dirt into his eyes.

He thought that I was there to slop sewage into his ditch.

For that's what he dealt with for years.
He lived in this dirty ditch of darkness for years.
All alone.

It was his home.

And, like he did with the others, he reached up to grab me.

He reached up with his nasty, enormous hand to grab me--to pull me down, to pull me in--and to devour me.

But, instead of trying to run, instead of running like others had done before--

I reached out to him as well.
I took his hand into mine,
and this amused him.

And, without him even knowing, he was fascinated
with me.

He was fascinated and simply amazed--that I wasn't
running.

And, so, he grabbed onto my hand,
then wrapped his dirty arms around my thin waist,
my soft, my white, my smooth, delicate waist,
and gently pulled me down to look at me some more.

To study me, and to look at me, some more.

I wrapped my lean arms around his neck.
I wrapped myself around his large and thick muscular
neck--and gently kissed his lips.

I kissed and I kissed and I kissed his dirty, dirty, black,
dark slimy lips--and fell deeper in love--than I had ever
been before.

Now we are together.
Happily in love, and always, and forever,
in our ditch of black, slimy darkness.

In love--

Forevermore.

The Runner Sled

"So, Bobby, what would you prefer, to die from drowning, or to burn to death?"

"Oh, I don't know…drowning I guess."

"Why?"

"Because it wouldn't be as painful."

"What makes you think that?"

"Uh, I think because it would be easier to gulp water than to have your lungs catch fire."

"But you might die from smoke inhalation first. What about that? That would make death less painful. If the fire didn't get to you first, the smoke would…and you would be dead already."

"Hey, you didn't say nothing about no smoke inhalation, Zack! That's not fair. Yourn't playing the game right."

"Yes I am. Stop being such a whiner. Whatever. Anyways…what would you rather die from…heatstroke, or freezing to death?"

"Um, freezing to death. Mommy says that to always dress warm in the winter because the cold can trick ya, and you could get what she calls hypothermia, and you would feel all warm and fuzzy before ya kicked it. So I guess I would rather freeze to death from the cold because when you die of heatstroke, you're hot all over, you're thirsty, you can't get away from the heat--which is something I hate--your body fries like ants under a magnifying lens, and, well…I just like the cold better."

"I guess that makes some sense…okay, now, what would rather die from, a gun shot wound, or a stab wound?"

"Um, geez, I don't know, I guess that depends on where you were stabbed or shot; if you were to die at the same amount of time, I would prefer a bullet to a knife being stuffed into my body. The bullet would be more of a surprise than a knife would be. I think the pain would be less too….c'mon, let's play something else. I'm sick of this game. It's boring. Let's go sledding instead!"

"Shit, no. Sledding is baby stuff. *I'm* fourteen. Goin' to be *fifteen* in two days. I want to continue this game. It's fun. I don't do sledding no more."

"Stop swearing. Mommy says you shouldn't swear, and besides, this game is boring…and scary, and Mommy said you…"

"*I* don't *care* what *Mommy* said. *I* don't have to do nothing with you if *I* don't want to. I'm older than you so I'm the boss. Besides, *Mommy* ain't here. And, get out of calling her Mommy. It's retarded. It's *Mom*. Yourn't four no more."

"Fine. If you don't want to do what Mommy, I mean *Mom*, asked you to do, I'm gonna tell Daddy that you don't want to follow orders, or play with me like you're s'pose to."

"*Wait!* Wait. No need to run and tattle. Just come back here. I'll go with you. Dad, not *Daddy*, don't need to know nothing. What hill do you want to go down?"

"Oh, cool! Zack, let's go down the steep one in front of the house. Can we? I betcha' that it's covered with ice. I'll go get the runner sled."

"Fine. I'll wait right here. Hurry up. Don't drag your ass."

"Don't swear!" Bobby said. Bobby ran to the barn to grab his sled that he had gotten for a Christmas present. Zack watched his little brother make his way through the snow--slipping and sliding along the icy shoveled path. Sighing, Zack kicked at a piece of ice. It went sailing along the path behind his little brother.

Zack hated Bobby. Mom always said that hate was such a terrible word, but it fit. Zack couldn't help it--he *hated* his kid brother. He always did his best to be nice to him. He tried to do things with him and pal around with him, but it was hard. Hard, because, Zack had always known that Bobby was the favorite. It was the truth. It was that way ever since Bobby had been born. Zack knew that fact from the very day Mom and Dad brought Bobby home from the hospital. *The parents* drooled all over the little wrinkly baby. Zack could never forget how Mom kept saying over and over how beautiful *this* boy was, and he remembered Dad saying that *this* one, *this* little boy, was going to make something of himself one day. Every now and again, those words that his parents said back then, and sometimes say now, still sting whenever he thinks about them.

Unfortunately, Zack, (at the mature age of fourteen-going-on-fifteen) knew that his nine-year-old brother was going to be the smarter one, already was, in fact. He was also the more athletic one, and he certainly was going to be the one that everyone wanted to be like and look up to. Mom and Dad bragged to family and friends about the many differences there were between their two boys. They did this as far back as Zack could remember. They did it all of the time! They would tell others about how Bobby was destined for great things. They would tell anyone willing to listen that Bobby's grades were terrific; that Bobby sang beautifully, and that when Bobby played the piano, he was *so* gifted, his music could bring tears to your eyes.

They would go on and on and *on* about how Bobby got Student of the Month, every month, and now his teachers and the principle at the elementary school were already making preparations to bump him up a grade, or maybe even two. Mom and Dad would tell everyone about how Bobby was definitely going to go far in life. And, if anyone dared to ask how their older son, Zack, was doing, if anyone in Zack's corner *dared* to challenge Mom and Dad, well, Zack--Zack would make a good farmer. That was the response--always the response. That's right. He would make a good simple farmer. That's what *he* was made for. And then they would glance his way with such regret and disgust in their eyes. Zack knew well enough by now not to make a fuss with anything *the parents* had to say about him. It wasn't worth the fight.

Besides, Zack thought, being a farmer was pretty cool. Farming it to make a living wouldn't be so bad. He liked living on the farm and tending to the animals. He liked doing hay. All of the chores that he did on a daily basis felt like such an accomplishment to him. He also noticed, and happily so, that all the chores he did helped tone him up, too. He knew that he had more power and a better physique than all of the other guys in his class. And, fortunately for him, Suzette noticed, as well. She may be a year older than he was, she may be Bobby's (and most embarrassingly so) Zack's babysitter, but she most certainly took notice. (The two of them had been secretly dating since the summer; Zack didn't want to even *think* about what *the parents* would do if they found out about that little gem.) It's just the way that his parents talked about farming that made him mad. They made farming out to be something bad. Christ! Dad's a farmer! Why was he so embarrassed about who his is and what he does? Zack would never understand his parents--he would never understand their distaste in him.

Bobby returned from the barn and was pulling his prized sled behind him. His face was beaming with delight. Zack could almost hear his mother's voice in his head saying, "Oh, Bobby, look how cute you look with your little rosy cheek! So cute, I could just *pinch* them right off of your face!" And then--in Zack's mind--he could literally see her rush by him, practically running him over in the process, to pinch Bobby's chubby cheeks and cover his face with kisses. Man--no matter how much time he spent with his little brother-- Zack could never fully enjoy himself or his brother's company as much as he knew he should. Somewhere, deep down, Zack *knew* that he should like Bobby. Everyone else liked him. Why didn't he?

"Whatcha' thinkin' 'bout, Zack?" Bobby asked. He was huffing and puffing--out of breath from his brief run--his little face was red and shiny in the winter sun; actually, to Zack, Bobby looked rather fat and disgusting, not cute at all. "Zack, you look like you were mad about something. Are ya mad?" Bobby's sled made a scraping sound as he gave it a final tug and it rested against his boot heel.

"Wha'? Oh, just nothin'. Grown up things. Stuff you wouldn't be interested in. C'mon, let's go and get this over with."

"Yeah! All right!" Bobby gave his runner sled a tug, and took off toward the front of the house to the hill, with his sled fishtailing behind him. The sound of its runners on the ice made Zack cringe. He followed slowly behind--his hands thrust deep into his pockets.

Bobby made it to the top of the hill, positioned himself with his belly down on the sled, put his arms on the snow on both sides of the sled, gave a push, and down he went. He was right--the snow had an ice-crust that allowed Bobby to sail down the hill with ease. The runners on his sled did not even break through the hard exterior into the soft underbelly of the snow.

Bobby reached the bottom of the hill and then sat up on his sled, "Hey, come down here and bring my sled back up for me," he shouted up to Zack, "I'm kinda tired and you're stronger than I am."

"Are you serious, Bobby? Are you *that* lazy that you can't drag it back up here yourself?"

"Plleeaassee?" Bobby shouted.

"FINE, you friggin' whiner!" Zack shouted back, and then reluctantly trudged down the hill. He knew that he better do what his little brother (the precious little prince) wanted, or Zack would never hear the end of it from his parents, later on. Sometimes, Zack wished Bobby would just disappear from existence.

Reaching his kid brother, Zack bent down and picked up the twine at the front of the sled, "Okay, get up, Bobby, I ain't gonna pull the sled up the hill with *you* on it. You're gonna have to walk."

"No, you can pull me up. I know you will. And, if you don't, I'll go and tell Mommy and Daddy that you ain't being nice to me."

"Are you kidding me? I walked all the way down here to listen to this! I walked down here to you and you have the *nerve* to ask me to pull you up. Get off!"

Bobby looked up at Zack, and by the look on his face, it appeared that Bobby was about to cry, something that he always did effortlessly to get his way. But, surprisingly, he softened his usual pout, simply smiled, and again lay his belly down on the sled.

"Hey, Zack," Bobby said, "Guess who I am?"

To Zack's surprise and then utter shock, Bobby proceeded to hump the sled while moaning Suzette's name over and over.

Zack's face grew hot and his heart began to pound ferociously in his chest. He had no idea that Bobby knew about him and Suzette! And to have

Bobby *act out* what he had obviously seen--Zack and Suzette doing it--was just too much to handle.

"What the *fuck* is the matter with you, you little asshole? I always knew you could be a little dick! What I do with Suzette is none of your *fuckin'* business!" Zack bent down and pulled the runner sled out from underneath Bobby--Bobby fell off of it in a huff. Zack immediately threw the sled, and it landed a few feet away, and then he effortlessly picked his little brother up by the front of his coat; Bobby's feet were dangling a few inches above the ground.

"Put me down, Zack. I'll scream. You know that I will. I'll scream so loud that everybody'll think that you're hitting me! You know I'll do it, Zack, and Mommy and Daddy will believe *me* over *you* like they always do. They *hate* you! And if you don't do what I say, I'll tell all there is to know about you and the babysitter, and you know very well that one word from me to Mommy and Daddy about it, and they will beat you 'til you're bloody and sore!"

Zack's breathing slowed and his muscles relaxed a bit. He blinked a few times to focus, slowly putting Bobby back down. He knew Bobby was right. He knew that he would get into a shitload of trouble if he didn't listen to what Bobby was threatening to do.

Zack wanted to kill the little prick. He really did. He wanted this kid to go away for good. Years of being in his little brother's shadow had taken its toll on his mind. If this little pipsqueak had never been born, Zack knew that his life would've been so much better. So much *simpler*. His mind was racing as he cleared his throat; the urge to cause bodily harm to Bobby was so intense, too intense. "Go. Get. You better go and get away from me, and get your fuckin' sled yourself, Bobby, 'fore I do somethin' that I can't take back."

Turning, Zack quickly walked away and began to climb back up the hill, toward the house.

Retrieving his sled, Bobby followed Zack up the hill. For fun, he decided to try, once more, to get Zack to pull it up the hill for him, "Zack, pull my sled up for me and let me ride on it while you do so."

Stopping in his tracks, Zack spun around to face his kid brother, "Christ, Bobby! What do you fuckin' *want* from me you little shi..."

"I want you to stop swearing, and I want you to do what I say--that's what I want."

***

Bobby left his runner sled next to Zack's body. He didn't want to touch it, anyway, because Zack left his blood and brains all over it. Typical stupid Zack--he was always *so* rude.

Bobby walked into the house and told Mommy and Daddy the truth about what had happened.

Bobby told them--Zack had lost control of the sled when he went down the icy hill.

Bobby told them--Zack was moving very, very fast on the sled, and that he hit his head really, really hard when he fell off.

Sobbing, Bobby told Mommy and Daddy that he was worried about Zack, and even though he wasn't completely sure, he thought that maybe, just maybe-- Zack might be dead.

Toothsome

So, on I-90 we were headed east,
little wifey's *incessant* nagging was driving me crazy.

"It's your fault we're going home so late!"
She said.
"It's *your* fault we missed my sister's wedding!"
She said.
"What the *hell's* the matter with you?"
She said.

She stomped her feet like a spoiled child,
in the midst of a tantrum.

Ugh, two hours of this was enough.

I saw a billboard sign that read--
'Your Favorite Restaurant!'
'*Anything* you want to eat and more!'
Exit 8.

I signaled and approached the off-ramp.

"Where are you going?"
She asked.
"We don't have time to *eat*!"
She shrieked.
"Jackie's *waiting*!'
She said.

"Screw Jackie."
I said.
"That damn mutt can wait."
I said.
"I'm hungry and I have to get out of this friggin' car."
I said.

She crossed her arms and pouted,
while I pulled into the parking lot.

"Are you coming in?"
I asked.

"I'm staying *right* here!"
She said.

"Fine, whatever."
I said.

I slammed the car door shut.

I found a booth at the far end of the eatery,
and seated myself.

"Hello, sir, what can I get you?"
The waiter asked.
"Anything you want."
He said.
"*Anything*."
He said.

His smile was as bright as the sun.

I laughed.
"Cook up my wife."
I said.
"Sauté *her* with some garlic and vegetables."
I said.
"A nice bottle of wine would be *swell*."
I said.

The waiter laughed.
"Coming right up!"
He said.

Fifteen minutes later,
my dinner was before me,
and, it was the best meal that I have ever had!

The vegetables were cooked to perfection.
The red wine was an *excellent* complement,
and the meat was so tender.

"Here is the check."
The waiter said.
"Everything has been taken care of."
He said.
"Enjoy your evening, and please do come again."
He said.

I paid my bill, and left a most deserving tip.

I walked outside and my car was gone,
and a taxi was waiting for me.
I climbed on in, and went home.

'Hellish crash on I-90 last night!'
The morning paper read.
'The car was a pile of burned ash.'
It read.
'No bodies.'
It read.

I burped.
I smiled.
I patted my stomach.

"Come on, Jackie."
I said.
"Let's go for a *rrriiide!*"
I said.
"Get in the car."
I said.
Jackie growled at me.
Stupid thing never liked me, I never liked him,
and I think he knew what I was after.

I picked him up by the scruff of the neck, and he bit me.
I threw him onto the backseat.

"Glad to see you again, sir."
The waiter said.

What a fantastic restaurant,
what a gracious waiter,
such a dashing smile.

Body Art

The day Jade Darling turned 18--she vowed that she would get a tattoo. She saved up what little money she was allowed to have and planned on getting a tattoo as a birthday present to herself. She loved art, body art, in particular, and never understood why her parents were so against it.

"Tattoos are disgusting," her mother said; but, yet, Mom didn't see anything wrong with getting her nose pierced at fifty-five, did she? Now, *that* was disgusting.

"When you turn eighty, you'll look in the mirror and think that your ugly, wasted, wrinkled skin just looks terrible," Jade's father said to her. "And, with a tattoo added to that at-death's-door-mix, you'll be embarrassed of yourself," he added, after taking a long gulp of beer. Yet, further contributing to his seventy-inch waist beer belly.

Jade had chosen not to listen to them anymore. Both of her parents had issues, both led terrible lives, and to Jade, they weren't experts on anything, least of all, the perfect body image.

Jade researched tattoo parlors in her area and took note of what her friends had told her. 'Look for credentials,' they said. 'Don't have a tattoo party in your own home,' they warned. 'Don't go to the tattoo artist's house, and pick a place that is well lit and clean.' Jade finally found one that she thought was a perfect fit. A tattoo parlor called "Exchange." She set up an appointment.

Exchange was an unusual name, but the history of the place was strong. It was licensed by the state of Massachusetts, and in business since 1990. It was well kept. Jade was very impressed.

Framed drawings hung on the white walls in Exchange, and books of art were displayed on four separate tables in every corner of the room for the customers to look through.

Jade had an idea of what she wanted: a single rose with black petals, a dark gray curvy stem with delicate thorns and leaves, and a light gray vine circling its way down the stem. She thought that a rose lacking color would represent her life perfectly. She wanted it to be approximately three inches long, two inches wide, and put on the lower left side of her back. Jade found just what she was looking for in one of the books. She brought the book up to the counter and pointed to the tattoo that she wanted.

"Perfect choice," the tattoo artist said--Spike was his name. "Do you want the exact size of this, or on a smaller scale?"

"Bigger," Jade said.

"Are you sure?" Spike asked.

"Totally. I want it to be about three inches long and two inches wide and put on the lower left side of my back."

"Okay. You're the one with the money. Let's go to the back."

Jade followed Spike down the hall toward the furthest room on the right. The sound of needles buzzing behind closed doors filled her ears. This was a reassuring sound, which satisfied Jade, and she felt that she had picked the right place.

"Sounds to me like you get a lot of business here," Jade said.

"Yup, we do," Spike answered, "Sundays are our slow days. You're lucky that you picked today to come in. Any other day of the week, and you'd be waiting several hours before you could even get back here to one of these rooms. Here we are," Spike gestured to the chair in the center of the room, "have a seat."

Spike took his seat at the desk and Jade sat down in the chair. To Jade, the chair she was in looked similar to a dentist's chair. In fact, upon further inspection, Jade concluded that it was, in fact, at one time, a dentist's chair. For a split second, she had a sinking feeling that she was in a dentist's office--ready to have a needle full of local anesthetic. She shivered.

"I know. You feel like you're in a dentist's office," Spike said. He laughed. "We pride ourselves on our sterile environment, and I gotta admit that our dentists' chairs give it that extra push. Okay, let's get down to business."

Spike scanned Jade's picture. Seconds later, the image of her soon-to-be tattoo stared back at her from the computer screen. With a couple of quick movements of his fingers on the keys, Spike enlarged the picture of the rose according to Jade's specifications, and then pressed the 'print' button. "Be right back," Spike said, and walked out of the room.

A minute later, Spike returned with what appeared to be tracing paper of Jade's rose in his hand.

"That's pretty cool," she said, "I didn't know that you print it out on tissue paper."

"Yup, it's something similar to tissue paper, I guess. It's interesting what we can do with technology these days. It wasn't twenty years ago or so where everything was traced by hand. Now, all we have to do is print it out, clean the area where you want the tat, slap it on, and needle away. Now, if you please, stand up for a second so I can recline the seat back flat."

Jade stood and Spike pressed the button on the chair and it snapped back. She lifted her shirt to expose her lower back and then lay down on her stomach.

"Yeah. Cool. Relax, and most importantly, do *not* move."

"All right. No problem." Jade said. "You don't have to worry about *me* moving, I've been wanting a tattoo for years. I want this perfect."

***

The pain was grating. To Jade, it felt like wasps stinging her over and over again in the same place. It was deep, hot and intense. The shading was worse than the outline because Spike had to put the shading on in a circular motion.

Jade was actually about to stop Spike from continuing, she couldn't take the pain anymore, but then he stopped on his own. He was done.

"Okay. All set. Take a look." Spike handed her a mirror.

"Oh, it's beautiful!" Jade said. "I'm so happy that I did this."

"That's what we like to hear. Don't be a stranger. Make Exchange your place to go when you are ready for you second tat," he winked.

Jade laughed, "I just got my first one. I don't think that I'll be getting a second one, or a third one for that matter, any time soon."

"That's what they all say. If you ask me, body art is an addiction. The first one is always just for you. It's personal. The ones you get later always represent something else. They could be for your friends, pets, parents--anything. Just wait. You'll see."

Jade followed Spike out to the front of the shop and paid the bill.

***

That night, she showed her parents. They weren't pleased.

"So, you were just that *stupid* enough to go and disfigure your body." her dad said. He belched and looked her up and down--pointing his finger at her, "I don't want to hear any *bitching* from your pissy little mouth in a year or two when you're sick of it and want it lasered off. I won't be paying for that shit."

"That looks so ridiculous!" Jade's mother said. Laughing, she twirled her nose ring with her thumb and forefinger, and then she put the tips of her fingers up to her nostrils and sniffed them. "You look trashy--makes you look like a nasty-ass slut."

Jade walked to her room and closed the door behind her.

If only she could do away with her parents' hurtful remarks. As far as she could recall, when they weren't hitting, pinching, or shoving her, they belittled everything she did. She often wondered why they even bothered to have her in the first place. No matter, she would be heading off to college in the fall, anyhow, and she definitely had chosen to be a campus resident.

Jade faced her back to her vanity mirror and lifted her shirt. She took off the gauze and examined her rose.

"How pretty. Perhaps I will get a second one, or a third, after all," she laughed. "But, unlike what that tattoo guy, Spike said, I don't think that I will *ever* get any tattoos to represent my parents or their lives."

Getting the tattoo made Jade feel empowered. It was something that she had chosen to do all on her own. No one demanded her to do it. It was through her freewill. She didn't wait for permission, and she didn't do it to please her negligent and abusive parents--like she did with everything else in her life. And perhaps, now, *hopefully*, they both would be so disgusted with her appearance and her boldness that they would leave her alone. She pulled down her shirt and got ready for bed.

She was wrong.　The tattoo just made them angrier.

***

The next day she skipped meeting up with her friends to spend the day in the park instead. She found the large boulder in the park that she always liked to sit on and climbed on top. The sun felt good on her skin, and to ease her physical pain, Jade let her mind drift to the more pleasant thought of her future.　She was excited about college.　She would pack up and leave this town. She knew that she had the strength within her to hold on for just a few weeks more.　She couldn't wait.

Yet, despite everything, however, these thoughts, as well as others, couldn't erase her sadness. Sitting there, she realized, that she would miss the boulder and this park, and that she would miss the town, as well. That was true. She did have a couple of good friends here that she didn't want to leave, but she just had to go--just had to. She felt that she had no other choice. She couldn't *wait* for that part of her life to begin.

Propping herself up on her elbows, Jade leaned back and then closed her eyes. Tears no longer flowed from them like they used to. The sadness and pain she felt all of these years was slowly being replaced by the excitement that she was indeed about to leave her parents forever.

"Hey, it's Jade, right? How you doing this morning? It's nice to see you again." Startled, Jade jumped and turned. It was Spike, the tattoo guy from Exchange.

"Oh, I'm sorry. Didn't mean to scare you. I just didn't expect anyone up here. When the weather is nice, this is where I go to eat breakfast before I go to work."

"That's okay," Jade said; "during the summer, I'm usually hanging out with my friends right about now, but, I kind of wanted to have some alone time...to think about going off to college...stuff like that. That's the reason why I am here."

"You don't need to lie. I see the real reason why you would want to be alone. You have some marks on your skin," he gestured to her neck. Jade pulled the top of her shirt up higher to her chin.

"Hey, it's okay," Spike said, he squatted down beside her and gently took her hands into his, and then pulled them down to her sides; "I know what it feels like to grow up in a shitty house--my parents were handsy."

Jade averted her eyes, "I never said that my parents did this to me...I'm quite clumsy."

"Listen," Spike said, "I know abuse when I see it. Just like I know that someone's first tattoo is the most meaningful. You don't need to feel embarrassed, and you should know that you have done nothing wrong to deserve any of this." Spike pointed to the bruises on her neck.

Suddenly, Jade realized that Spike was being sincere. She realized that he was just trying to show her that he cared. And then, surprisingly, Jade did something that she never had done before--she told another human being of the kind of hell that she had been living in.

When she had finished, the world around them seemed to grow quiet. Jade could only hear her heart pounding away in her chest. She felt that she had made a mistake confiding in a man that she barely knew. He answered her concern quickly.

"Don't feel like you made a mistake telling me your story. Mine is very similar. Both of my parents were nasty beings and I made damn sure that they suffered for what they did to me and to my sister."

"What do you mean?" Jade asked.

"Like I said to you yesterday when you got your tat. The first piece of body art is for the individual getting it. The ones that follow are for other things in your life. It could represent someone you lost, loath, want to forget, anything that you want it to be, it can be. Whatever. At Exchange, we artists come from colorful backgrounds, so to speak. All of us have had traumatic experiences occur in our lives, and as a result, all of us at Exchange have come together and created a place where we help each other, and help the people that come into our shop, as well."

"I don't understand what you're saying," Jade said. "How do you help people?"

"Exchange creates happiness for her customers. She also gets rid of any problems that customers may have, and sees to it that those problems are never able to hurt anyone ever again. She is Mother."

Jade swallowed and cleared her throat. "What? A mother? I...I still don't get what you are saying."

Spike grabbed Jade's hands once more, giving them a little squeeze. "Do you want your parents to leave you alone? Do you want them to stop? It can all be arranged. You would never have to deal with them anymore. You wouldn't have to leave this town--if you didn't want to. You wouldn't have to run away."

"Who said that I was running away? I wouldn't call going off to college running away," Jade said; but as soon as those words left her lips, she even knew that what she was saying was a lie. It was what she was doing, and she knew it. She was running away. The local college had all that she needed.

Jade had to admit--she was intrigued. She never thought that she could be rid of her parents. Besides, deep down, she knew that no amount of distance would ever really keep her parents at bay. Nothing could.

"I don't know what you are getting at, Spike, but, yes, I do want them out of my life...but how?"

Spike smiled. "Is there a friend's place that you can stay at tonight? A place where your parents won't go looking for you? Or care?"

Jade thought for a moment, "When my parents get mean, or 'handsy,' as you put it...um...I usually go stay at my friend's house for a couple of nights. I can't face Mom and Dad a couple of days after that *stuff* happens, anyways." Jade quickly looked away--she was embarrassed.

"Good. Good. Go, do that, and leave everything to me," Spike quickly kissed her cheek and then got up to go. "I am your friend, Jade. Everyone at Exchange is your friend. We will help you. *She* can help you. We will take care of everything. Don't you worry."

"Okay," Jade said, "but after tonight…what do I do?"

Spike looked at his watch, "Meet me at the shop at this time tomorrow. I will show you how Exchange can help."

Spike jumped off of the boulder and walked away. Jade felt an uneasy excitement rise up in her. Could she trust Spike? A stranger? She would have to wait until tomorrow morning to find out.

***

Jade spent the night at her girlfriend's house. Her friend's parents welcomed her in like they always did. Unbeknownst to Jade, everyone in the small town had the impression that Jade was being mistreated at home. People talked. People knew.

The following morning Jade walked into Exchange and saw Spike at the counter cashing out a customer.

"Good morning, Jade, I'm glad you came in."

"Hi, Spike. I did like you suggested. I stayed at a friend's house last night and came straight here this morning."

"I know. Yes, I know, and that's a great first step in the right direction. So, now, are you ready to begin your new life? Are you ready for that fresh start?"

"Uh, I am," Jade said, but then shook her head; "I can't get one while I'm still near my parents, though. That will never happen. Can't happen."

"Yes it can. Come on. Follow me."

Jade followed Spike down the hall--the same hall she had been down just two days ago. He walked passed the room that she had gotten her tattoo in, and stopped at a door at the end of the hall. Spike grabbed a key out of his pocket to unlock the door. They both stepped inside.

The room felt cold, and when Spike flipped the light switch, Jade saw that the room was filled with boxes and crates, and there were hooks of various sizes hanging from the ceiling.

"Are we in some sort of freezer?" Jade asked.

"Yes, of sorts," Spike replied. "Exchange used to be a butcher shop. We have, for obvious reasons, modified it for the tat use, but we all agreed that this walk-in freezer would come in handy and be a good thing to keep."

"What's in the boxes?"

"Ink. Drawings. Supplies. Equipment. Everything we need to make our business a success."

Jade was curious, "Why did you bring me back here? What does this place have to do with me?"

"See those?" Spike pointed to two boxes to the left side of the room. "All of what is in those boxes was finished earlier this morning. Inside is fresh ink and drawings generously donated. Want to take a look?"

"Um, sure." Jade walked to the boxes and saw that "Jade Darling" was written on them. She turned to look at Spike, confused, "Why is my name on these?"

"Just open them. Go on."

Jade opened the first box. In it were tiny bottles filled with the most brilliant, vibrant colors. There were hundreds of colors of varying degrees. Colors that Jade didn't think could even exist.

In the second one, stacks of drawings filled the box, art that Jade had never seen before. Not even artwork that she looked at in books could compare to what she saw in this one simple box.

"These are gorgeous. What talent! I have never seen such beauty. Who mixed these colors? Who did this art?"

"Our people," Spike said. He walked over to Jade and took her hands into his, "Our artists did these, and, they did it with *your* help."

"What do you mean they did it with my help? I don't understand? This is the second time that I have been here. How could *I* possibly help create this beautiful work?"

Spike smiled, "With the pain and suffering that you have endured at the hands of your parents. That is how all of this was created."

"I still don't get it."

Spike reached into the first box, picked up several bottles of ink, and carefully handed them to her.

"Jade, these colors were created from the blood and bodies of your parents--created right in this very room." Jade gasped and the ink nearly fell out of her hands. Spike smiled and steadied her. His eyes were warm and compassionate.

"And these drawings," Spike picked up a few of the samples, "these drawings were drawn by our Exchange artists who sat in your house last night, and with empathy toward you, with love *for* you, they drew them. They could feel your pain in that house. They could feel your parents' hatred. You only have to look at what is in these boxes to realize that you are special."

Jade put the ink back in the first box; she couldn't believe what she was hearing. She didn't know whether to laugh or cry--scream or shout.

"Is this for real?" Jade heard herself say. "This, this beauty was…created from *me*?"

"Yes," Spike said. He smiled. "Jade, you are a beautiful person. You did not find Exchange--Exchange found you."

Spike gestured to the boxes, "Jade, this is *you*."

***

He walked up to the counter at Exchange. He was a thin, young man, wearing dirty, dark clothes and despite his every effort--he simply could not hide the sadness in his eyes. He handed the girl at the counter the tattoo samples book, with the page of the design that he had chosen opened up for her to see, she took the book from his hands.

"Hi, welcome to Exchange," she said, she was a pretty girl. She had such warmth and love in her smile--something that he simply was not used to.

She looked down at the artwork that he had chosen, "A beautiful piece," she said. "I'm so flattered that you picked this one--I made this myself. Thank you! So, c'mon then, this way, follow me, and let's get started. Trust me, you're going to love it."

The young man followed Jade Darling down the hall.

Newsreel: Vampires Prefer Vino!

Concerned Citizens:
May I have your attention, please?

The world is full of disease--
Hepi A.
Hepi B.
Hepi C.

And HIV.
And AIDS.

Vampires are among the undead,
but, they too, must imbibe wisely!

And, since disease is everywhere,
the Vampire prefers vino to blood.
(Which is why we don't see Vampires anymore!)

Vampires have adjusted to their surroundings,
like, we, among the living, have done.

Now, Vampires are very particular about whom they
drink from.

Very selective.

They'd rather ravage liquor stores than the living.
(Do you blame them?)

Wine. Works. Fine.

So, don't you worry,
Mommy and Daddy Vampire.

Little Johnny will be all right!
He may be a bit skinny.
A teeny-tiny bit sluggish.
But, he does get *some* supplemental nourishment from
wine!

And always remember good folks--
a drunken undead kid is better than no undead kid at
all!

Manic Mind

"Yeah, sorry about that. Sorry I didn't get back to you sooner. Been busy. I have a lot of projects going on right now...lawnmowers, tractors, a couple of trucks, four-wheelers, cars...you name it. Thanks for coming in, though. Here, have a seat. So, yeah, your truck is taking longer than I had expected. It has more problems with it than I had anticipated. The whole front-end is shot...shit the bed. I'm guessing that it should be ready and running in about two weeks or so...what? What was that? Oh, I know, I know, I agree...being left in the dark really bugs the hell out of me, too...*really* bugs me...you have no idea. I apologize for that, meant to get back to you sooner...should've called. I'm serious, I'm sorry...but...but...left in the dark...dark...that reminds me...listen. *I'm* not talking about being *literally* left in the dark, here, you know, I mean...I'm talking about being left in the dark *emotionally*. Being literally left in the dark, well, that's actually comforting. You can't see anything, or hear anything. What you only hear are voices of the ones who love to communicate with you. The world is quiet...except for...for...do you know that the clouds...all the clouds...are a part of the color spectrum...um...wait...where was I? Never mind.

"When your intuition tells you, *nags you* that something is amiss, you can't help but feel insignificant to your so-called loved one. To be told that it's none of your business, or to be told *continually* so, that you're simply being paranoid, sucks. And, when that day finally, finally, comes--when you *finally* get a part of the truth--reality hits you and you sink into a depression that (without the help of alcohol or prescription meds or both) you just can't shake. You feel like a total piece of shit. My favorite combo, by the way, is four pills of antidepressants, and a strong rum and coke. A couple glasses of wine take the edge off too. So does weed. I don't necessarily like the hard stuff though--it really screws with my mind. Do you know that the world is a part of the time-space continuum?   There is a large pendulum in the sky that Father Time controls.

"But anyways, I remember when I finally got most of the truth. It took months of nagging on my part to get that much. I do admit though, that scheming, eavesdropping, and spying helped a bit, too. I was shocked. It was all that I could think about. I couldn't eat or sleep. I know that sounds so cliché, like something off of a TV show, but it's a matter of fact. I kept thinking about it. I didn't want to believe any of it! They spent more time together than I thought they did. All those business trips…all a bowl-full of crap. I even expressed my thoughts and inner feelings about the matter in a letter to my wife, but the security that I felt in her response to my letter--that heartfelt letter-- didn't last too long. She was supportive--for a change-- she offered up a little bit of what she was thinking-- surprisingly--but I still couldn't help shake the idea that I just wasn't getting the whole truth.

"The WHOLE TRUTH is what I desire. Man, what is so damn wrong with that, right? Mother Nature supports the whole truth. Mother Nature KNOWS that the world is flat in some places. Why wouldn't I think that my wife, the love of my life, my *soul mate*, the mother of my *kids*, would not want to tell me what was going on behind my back?

"And, holy shit, what I heard about the whole ordeal was *nothing* compared to the entire story. And all of that came after his death. When *she* was devastated. When his spirit came to me...but people never die, you know...they just go for a ride on the big pendulum in the sky.

"The texting is what started this whole friggin' thing, you know. My wife was texting him daily. And he--her. Never mind the fact that I asked her, every day, what was up, or had anybody called her, emailed her, or, whatever. It was a simple question that always went unanswered. This began my suspicions. Or, what my wife called my 'paranoia.'

"Let me tell you...they had been friends for years. Before I even married her, I knew that at times I would be the third wheel to them. But, I knew this going in. But, what I *didn't* know was at what *expense* I would be the third wheel...did you know that the wheel at the center of the earth has seven spokes for each day of the week? Why doesn't it have twelve? There are twelve months in the year. Why doesn't it have *twelve*? That doesn't make any sense! There is only room on this planet for ONE wheel. Let alone *three*.

"To think about what had been going on for nearly twenty years still hurts. Can't get over it. Doctor tells me that I have to. *That* bitch can go to Hell! (If there is such a place. Christians want you to believe this. It's nothing more than a scare tactic.) Like *she* ever had marital issues. Bitch. Therapy doctor bitch... *'Stan, you need to get past this moment in your life,'* she's always saying to me in that insufferable, shrill voice of hers... *'Stan, you need to keep taking your meds,'* she says...I'll take those meds...and I'll shove 'em up her ass...that's what I'll do. She'll probably like it though, knowing her! Whore. *'Stan, you're not cooperating,'* she says. Therapists are so overrated, man. *'Stan, Stan, Stan.'* Shit...SHE NEVER SHUTS THE FUCK UP! She just better watch herself...no pendulum ride for her.

"There are *thousands* of cosmos in the universe. We, the human race, ride on one and only one. There are endless possibilities. You jump on the spectrum cloud to the pendulum and take a swing. If you get to the cosmos, you can visit with Father Time. If you miss that pendulum, and you fall, you better mother fuckin' *pray* that you land on one of those seven wheel spokes. Because, if you don't, and you land between one of them instead, Mother Nature won't be so nurturing. She has to make sacrifices, too, you know.

"Primary colors: red, yellow, and blue...make white. That is why clouds are on the spectrum. They are white. Innocent. *The color of innocence.* If you manage to get on one, you were a good person in this life. If you go toward that pendulum and the swing is in your favor, you're set. If you reach for it and Father Time swings it the opposite way, you are *not* in his favor. He will laugh at you. You are *screwed*. In the *ether* is where you'll land. No man's land. Land of black and pain...*ether*.

"Ether is the connection between Father Time's world and Mother Nature's world. This is where they conduct their meetings about who falls between the spokes, and who gets to ride that awesome pendulum in the cosmos. Ether is also the place where these two Gods have *sex*. Ha! Isn't that something...that's when we here on Earth have thunderstorms...when Father Time and Mother Nature have sex in the ether. Not everyone knows that. The place of black and pain for our souls--is the place of *sex* for the Gods. The irony!

"I began to realize that I had a problem (what those 'normal' people call a problem, anyway) after our third child was born. I'm telling you, man, that kid had *horns*! Apparently, horns only *I* could see. I was diagnosed manic. Personally, I don't see it as a problem. I just simply see the world with *honest* eyes. I see it for what it is. Honest eyes, is what I have. Honest eyes. My mind is fresh and alert. Having my third precious little one, even though he had horns and a tail, just opened me up to the *entire* world. Not just what the typical human eye sees. I don't mask what I say to others like everyone else does. They call it babbling. *'Stan, stop babbling. You are always babbling.'* Blah, blah, blah, mother fuckin' BLAH...fuckers always got to say something, don't they?

"The nightmares that plague people are actually the truth trying to come forth and set you *free*. Actually...they are not nightmares...that's a wrong choice word. When you have these 'nightmares' it is actually at this part in your sleep that you are connected to the spirit world. The spirit world is trying to communicate with you. Having children only intensified this connection for me.

"When he died (the asshole, her lover) my wife was so distraught. She even asked me if I had anything to do with his death. Wait! What? What the fuck's up with that? I told her the truth. I told her that I had *no* part in his death and that his time was up. Plain and simple. Of course...she did not believe me. She divorced me and had me institutionalized. My children visited me on weekends. I was there for about a month, maybe two...maybe three...or more...I don't remember exactly, and let out on good behavior, and for the fact that I was a good patient and took my meds...shit like that. Those meds made me feel all wrong. I lost touch with the cosmos, and with the Gods. I couldn't see the pendulum anymore. Or the wheel. The planet no longer had flat spots. The primary colors went dull, almost non-existent. I stopped taking my medication after I got out of that shithole. That's why Doctor Bitch is always nagging me...Doctor Bitch Cunt.

"I didn't kill him. I do admit that I was quite happy that he died in that car crash, wrapped his car tight around a tree, all mangled up and shit, but that was simply Mother Nature's way of taking care of things. Mother Nature was overdue for a romp in the ether with her ever-faithful Father Time. She *needed* a worthless, sacrificial, piece-of-shit-soul to take up there with her. Thank goodness for Her! It wasn't *my* fault he was being an asshole and driving recklessly. I played no part in it. I guess his car malfunctioned, or some shit like that, or whatever. If you don't want me to fix your car, don't bring it to my fuckin' shop. It's as simple as that. You go sniffing around my woman, don't expect me to play nice. Simple as that. I had no intention of killing him. He can go fuck himself. Even after I found out that he and my wife were lovers. Even after I found out that the kids weren't even my kids! I didn't kill him. Lovers! Isn't that something...though we're not together anymore, she still brings her vehicle to my shop for maintenance. I charge her nothing. I do it out of love and respect for my kids. Well, I still feel that they're mine, anyway.

"I hope her car doesn't break down somewhere. It just might! Shit happens. Man...that pendulum is absolutely beautiful. Look! See that gold sparkle! See it out the window? See it? Oh, the wondrous colors. My, my, my. Fucking Beautiful...

"So, yeah...I do not like being left in the dark, either. Figuratively speaking. Like I said, your truck will be ready in a couple of weeks."

It's Blood-Bath-Time

Carly was distraught about the demons,
she said they wanted to slit her wrists.
Little men who danced on the edge of the bathtub,
taunting her with their little razors,
while she shaved her legs.

Carly said the demons were grotesque,
a dripping mixture of green and brown flesh.
They popped up out of the drain when she slid into the
water--they reeked of the sewers below.

I thought she needed help.
Reluctantly, she agreed with me.
We went to see a shrink.

He prescribed some meds,
but, they didn't work.
Carly's bathtub demons still came a-calling.

I came home from work one day.
The house was cold and dark.
I called for my wife--

Tick-tock.
Tick-tock.
Tick-tock.

Of the clock--answered back.

My heart thumped hard in my chest.
"C-C-Carly?"

I walked toward the bathroom,
the hallway stretched on for miles,
the bathroom door looked small and distant.

I held my breath.

I slowly turned the knob,
my hand was trembling,
I pushed the door open wide.

Carly was dead,
her wrists were slit.

I screamed.

I drew closer to the tub,
wanting to take her into my arms,
to take her out of that rose-red water.

That's when I heard a noise!

"Carly!" I said,
believing she was still alive,
needing for her to be still alive.
I went to shake her,
and I stopped short.

Shrill and distant laughter reached my ears.

Warbling--bubbling--roiling--boiling--
coming up from the water,
climbing up from the water,
swimming up from the water,
the laughter drew closer to the bloody surface.

Out popped the little demons.
Thirteen in all--gleaming razors in their hands.

They jumped onto the edge of the tub,
I fell backward onto the floor,
grinning, they jumped on top of me.

Oh, my Carly, my sweet, sweet Carly.
I believe you now.

Richard Rose I Repeat

-1900-

It had been a devastating week for the small New England town. The unexplained deaths were mounting, and the remaining residents were scared to come out of their homes at night. The staggering number of corpses--ninety-nine as of this moment--had been found for six nights straight--hidden in trash, in back alleyways, behind the local market, buried under dung heaps behind barns--all drained of blood.

Richard had never been witness to such trauma. He read the newspaper article several times over to really grasp the issue at hand. He couldn't believe the news. But, despite all that had been happening, however, Richard could not deny himself his weekly trip to the corner liquor store.

Richard was a hard man to frighten. He was the type of man who always admitted to everyone who knew him that he had never been afraid of anything his entire life. When his parents died--he did not shed a tear. When his sister jumped from the bridge ten years ago--he did not bat an eyelash. Nothing could get in the way of his own happiness. Nothing. The past week was no exception.

No, Richard was *not* self-centered, he just was the type of man that when things came his way, he took them at face value. His philosophy of life was a simple one: what was meant to be--was what was meant to be.

His parents' deaths were just another part of the cycle of life. His sister's suicide, too, was simply the unfortunate circumstance of a weak mind. Nothing could change Richard's philosophy. He would do and think whatever he wished. No man, no woman, or any other living being for that matter--could change the way he spent his time.

As Richard directed his black stallion up the paved street and then beyond the park toward the corner store, he noticed that the night was very quiet. Which was to be expected, considering, but--a somewhat different, deeper feeling had now reached his senses. No cricket could be heard. Not an owl sounded through the trees. The nearby brook was barely audible. Even the warm breeze listlessly moved through the air. The only sound to be heard was the low, rhythmic breathing of his horse underneath him, and its hooves methodically hitting the pavement.

Richard swore under his breath as he approached the store for its windows were dark. The one thing that he depended on--was closed like the rest of the town. As he pulled on the reins in the middle of the street, deciding what to do with the rest of this dismal night, a flicker of red perched upon the store step caught his eye.

He rode up to the curb in front of the store, dismounted, and tied his horse to a lamppost. He blinked a couple of times. He could not believe what he was seeing. She was alone. The full moon shown bright on her soft body--her red satin dress moved silently and hypnotically on the breeze.

Richard walked toward her--his eyes fixated upon her. The moonlight cast a silver glow on her fair complexion. To him, she was so beautiful, it was as though she was glowing from *within*. Her slender body sat erect on the curb, her delicate hands were folded neatly in her lap, and her wavy black hair hung loose down to her waist, swaying gently in the spring air.

Her delicate form sat there motionless like a lady out of a painting. On all of his weekly runs to the store--*this* was the first time that he had ever seen her. And, considering what had been happening during the week, all of the deaths, all of those bodies, his surprise to see such a beautiful creature intensified. Her unlikely presence greatly induced his interest in her.

As Richard approached she looked up at him with her pale blue eyes and smiled.

"Hello." She said. Her sultry voice was low and musical. It was no more than a whisper--but it carried to his ears effortlessly.

"Hello." Richard said. "What brings you out here at night all by your lonesome? It is very odd for a woman to be out like this, and, considering what has been going on recently, even more so." He carefully sat down on the step next to her.

"The full moon brought me out." She said. "I *simply* could not resist. I enjoy a full moon. You can see as far as you possibly can...almost like it is midday." She looked up at the sky and sighed.

Richard laughed. "I wouldn't really say that a full moon is as bright as the sun," he said, "but, I guess it comes close. So, if you do not mind me asking, what is your name?"

"Rose."

"Well, hello, Miss Rose. I'm Richard."

"Richard? Well, it is very nice to meet you, Richard." Rose brought forth her hand--he took it and brought it to his lips. He could not help but notice how cold it was.

"Are you cold?" He asked. "Here." With a grunt, he proceeded to take off his overcoat. She stopped him.

"No, no thank you, I am not cold. I just ate and a full stomach always warms me." She quickly changed the subject, "What brings you out here?" Rose studied him. He was indeed handsome. Unusually so. His eyes were dark like the earth after a hard rain. His curly hair was very light, almost white. His skin had a warm, creamy-colored hue. He was wearing a black suit, black overcoat, and a simple white dress shirt underneath. He was a sight to behold.

"I am out this way every week," he said, "I give this store good business." Richard chuckled.

"Really? I, myself, am out here regularly; I admit that I do enjoy my red wine, but this, I must say, is the first time that I have ever seen *you*. What about your wife?" She smiled, "Wouldn't she rather have you at home with her? And, what about all of the deaths here in town, aren't you scared?"

He laughed. It was deep and echoed in the quiet air, "I'm not married, pretty lady," Richard smiled, "I am but a simple bachelor. And...I should ask you the same...*why* is a lovely woman, such as yourself, out here on the curb in front of a liquor store of all places?"

Rose's heartbeat quickened in her chest. Giggling, she said, "I am a strong person...I can take care of myself. I'm not worried about what lurks around at night. I came out here for my beverage." To know that this young man was single and sitting next to her was perfect. She could not ask for better luck.

"Where are you from?" She asked. "Do you live here in town? I know everyone in this place, and yet, I have never seen *you* before."

"Yes, I have lived here all of my life. Who needs to leave? So full of opportunities--and *many* interesting people."

Rose blinked her big almond-shaped eyes-- trying to recall if she had seen this young man before-- she could not place him. But, she soon found that it simply did not matter. She slid closer to him to get a better look at his fine features.

The two sat for a few moments in silence. Rose, casually looking up at the night sky, and Richard, looking at the lovely young lady sitting next to him. He could not get over the fact that she was here by herself. To have a woman--*a woman*--as fearless as himself out alone in the dangerous night with a killer on the loose was invigorating.

This was the first time that he had ever felt like this. This chance meeting with this peculiar young lady was perfect. In just this short amount of time Richard sensed that this woman had the ability to change everything within his very existence, and quite possibly, could make him a very happy man.

Rose felt similar excitement rise within her. To have a young man, unmarried, handsome, respectful, coming to her, and making her feel wonderful about herself in such a small span of time was amazing.

The silence of the night intensified the pleasure for these two individuals. To know that no one was out watching, or listening, made the desire to be together undeniable.

Grabbing Richard's left hand, Rose gave it a reassuring squeeze, and brought it up to her lips. Richard moved in, wrapping his right arm around her waist and gently bringing her closer to him. He leaned forward and passionately kissed her on her cool lips. She moaned. Her breath was sweet against his skin. Her breathing grew rapid.

Breaking from their embrace, Richard hastily took off his overcoat, and spread it out on the sidewalk. He laid her out on the coat, and then made love to her like he had never done to any other woman before.

Richard felt amazing to Rose. This was *exactly* what she had longed for. This was *precisely* what she had come out into the night in search of. The power of the night, the full moon, the excitement of being in a village wallowing in such turmoil, brought her to ecstasy.

When Rose thought that she could take no more, when she thought that her whole body, her mind, her spirit, all full of excitement, could not endure any longer, Richard gave her one more surprise. This man, this wonderful, beautiful, powerful man, took his warm lips from her cool mouth, bent his head until his mouth rested upon her soft neck, and, punctured her supple flesh with his teeth.

Richard drank Rose's warm life from her firm body. Drank until he was full. His feeding could be heard through the still night air.

When he was finished with her--Richard lifted himself up off of Rose. He adjusted his clothing, grabbed hold of his overcoat from underneath Rose's lifeless body, and then yanked it out from under her like one would swipe a tablecloth from underneath dinner dishes in a parlor trick. Her body rolled to the right and settled inches from the store door. Wiping the remnants of her blood from his mouth with a handkerchief taken from his pants pocket, Richard stepped over her lifeless body, and walked away.

Rose's body was found by the owner of the liquor store the next morning.

-2000-

It had been a horrible week for the small New England town. The unexplained deaths were mounting, and the remaining residents were scared to come out of their homes at night. The staggering number of corpses--ninety-nine as of this moment--had been found for six nights straight--hidden in trash, in back alleyways, behind the local market, found down embankments beside the roads--all drained of blood.

Richard had never been witness to such trauma. He read the newspaper article several times over to really grasp the issue at hand. He couldn't believe the news. But, despite all that had been happening, however, Richard could not deny himself his weekly trip to the corner liquor store.

Headlines

"Hear Ye,"
"Hear Ye,"
"Read all about it…"

"Hot off the presses…"

BOY DIES OF BACTERIAL INFECTION.

SHOWERHEADS ARE FULL OF GERMS.

STAPH INFECTIONS ON THE RISE.

WIPE DOWN YOUR SHOPPING CART HANDLES.

THE KILLER KEYBOARD.

DISINFECT YOUR DOORKNOBS.

CLEAN YOUR COUNTERTOPS THOUROUGHLY.

BEWARE! THE KITCHEN SPONGE: BACTERIA BREEDER.

GET YOUR CHILD VACCINATED.

DON'T VACCINATE THE KIDS.

CHILDREN: THE DISEASE CARRIERS.

"This just in…"

MILLIONS DIE OF SANITIZER OVERDOSE.

HUNDREDS LEFT WITH SUPPRESSED IMMUNITY.

DEAD DISEASES BACK WITH A VENGEANCE.

SUPERBUG: THOUSANDS DEAD.

SUICIDES ON THE RISE.

HEALTH NEWS: HAND SANITIZER UNSAFE-- FULL OF BACTERIA.

The Queen Conch

"Yes, the shell is very pretty. Thank you for noticing! It sits on the nightstand by my bed, here, right here. Every night, I put my glass of water next to it, and then my eyeglasses.

"The shell is called a queen conch. Ha! I bet you didn't know that, now, did you? It's mostly pearly pink in color, and smooth to the touch on the inside, but is butterscotch-tan with these horn-like thingies on the outside. Look. See? I guess that you can say that it's about the size of a man's fist, or bigger? Yeah…it's bigger. The biggest point, the point on the end of my shell, is sharp…or is it the front? Oh, I don't know. Either way, I think that it is perfect. It has no flaws, except one, and crisp, wavy lines. It is perfect, well…almost. It's the last thing I see before my head hits the pillow each night.

"I like my shell. I find it amazing that it was a part of nature. Don't you think so? Simply, amazing. Made by a single snail gliding its way across the ocean floor. How long did it take for that shell to form? Years? How old was the snail? Fifty? One hundred? Who knows? And, just how long did it take for some fisherman to come along and kill it? Just seconds? I have so many questions. It just goes to show you that life is so precious, and that you should *never* take it for granted.

"I have many shells now. All different kinds, really. All beauties. I guess that one could say that I'm an avid collector of them, right? I've lost count, actually. When I was a little girl I always wanted shells. I looked for them in the woods, on the lawn, anywhere I thought one might possibly be. But, no luck. Shells don't grow where I grew up. No--it took me until I was in my twenties to finally get my hands on some. And--I never looked back. I have shells in every room of the house. They have become a part of the décor. But, as many as I have, I still have a hard time giving them up as gifts. Don't get me wrong, I do give them away…but reluctantly so. And, I only give them to family members so I can always visit with them when I visit the family.

"I'll never give up my queen conch, though. Never. Never. Never…

"My queen conch is cool to the touch. Whenever I pick it up and put it to my ear I swear that I hear the ocean. I can almost convince myself that I'm on the beach, and that the coolness of the shell is actually the ocean gently caressing my cheek. I can feel the hot sun on my body, the salt water on my lips, and the sea breeze upon my face. Just lovely.

"But, I can't go to the sea anymore…and I don't know why. It's not allowed, I guess…but…at least I have my queen conch, though…

"Robert hates my shell. I think that he dislikes all of them, really. He complains that I have too many, and that they are becoming dust collectors. I don't know what to do. I simply don't want to get rid of any. And, I don't know how to stop his bitching.

"Do you know, that on nights when I can't sleep, I sit up in bed and hold my cool shell in my hands? I love looking down at it. Its brightness in the dark room is so comforting to me. It is *radiant* in my cupped hands. And then I look at him…Robert. You know, he disgusts me sometimes. Snoring. Mumbling. Passing gas. Sleeping away. I put my shell to my ear and listen to its gentle voice whisper to me. Mercifully, it drowns out all of *his* sounds.

"Why doesn't he like it like I do? Do you know why he doesn't like it? You would tell me why he doesn't like it if you knew why, right? Robert's the one who gave it to me in the first place. How could he not like it? My shell is perfect! It never argues with me. It agrees with everything that I say. And, I agree with everything it whispers to me. We're best friends…

"One morning while Robert was at work, his damn cat jumped up onto the nightstand, knocking my shell to the floor. I screamed out, swatted her off of the nightstand, and picked the shell up. And what did the cat do? Nothing! She didn't even care. The bitch didn't even *realize* what she had done. Stupid animal. She just stared up at me, then went and jumped up on the bed, and then started to groom herself. Ugh, I hate cats…ass-lickers. Anyway, my shell was chipped! I couldn't believe it. *Chipped!* The chip was so small that I couldn't find the piece on the bedroom floor, at first. It literally took me hours to find it. And, all the while, that bitch of a cat was still in the same place on *my* side of the bed--of all places--licking her *ass*. How much time does a cat need to lick its ass? C'mon now, you bitch, it's *clean*! Talk about obsessive. Quit enjoying yourself with all that ass licking all the time. Christ!

"Anyway…the chip was hardly noticeable…but *that* is *not* the *point*. *I* knew that the chip was there, and *I* knew it was now flawed, and *I* knew that *I* had to fix it somehow! So I ran into the garage and rummaged through the drawers of my husband's worktable, luckily found some glue, and glued the piece back on. I did a pretty good job of it, too. See…you can barely see the crack…

"Afterward, I gave my queen conch a kiss, very carefully put it back in its place, and then I killed the cat.

"When Robert came home from work that afternoon, naturally, he had asked where the cat was…she always greeted him when he got home. I lied to him and told him that I had opened the back door to take the garbage out and the damn thing slipped passed me. He believed me. That cat had done that so many times in the past that I didn't have to work that hard to convince him…

"I didn't think that I needed to tell him that I broke the cat's neck and threw it into the furnace. She barely put up a struggle, really. It was easier than I thought it would be, actually. By the way, have you ever seen fur light up in a furnace? The flame burns a bright orange and you can hear the fur just sizzle right off! It's awesome--let me tell you. If you never had the chance to do so, try it sometime, you won't be disappointed, I assure you! Oh, and when the cat's body caught fire, you should've *heard* the pops and gurgles it made! Pretty cool. It was so noisy, it even sounded like the cat was still alive...huh...you know what...come to think of it...maybe she was...how interesting! I couldn't stay that long though, the flesh started to smell something awful, so, unfortunately, I had to close the furnace door because I was starting to gag...

"Well, anyway, my shell is just lovely. I finally figured out how old it is, too. Do you want to know? Of course you do. It's one hundred and twenty years old! Can you *imagine*? What? How do I know? Well, it told me so. So intelligent it is. My queen conch also whispered to me that it misses the snail that created it. Oh, now isn't that just the saddest thing that you've ever heard? My shell told me that some ruthless fisherman was having a beach party and grabbed more conch and lobster than he needed, and my shell and its snail were simply tossed aside uncooked! Do you know that snails can live out of the water for almost twenty-four hours? Oh my God! The poor thing *literally* baked in the hot sun while my shell looked helplessly on. My shell told me that it tried its best to shield its helpless snail from the hot sun, but, in the end, my queen conch couldn't do *anything* to save its snail! Oh, I am so sorry...this part of the story always brings tears to my eyes. Give me a second...you have a tissue? Thank you...okay...okay...I can continue now.

"After the party was over my Robert came by, yanked the dead snail out, and gave me the conch shell as a gift. Even though the snail met with a tragic end, tragic, tragic end, I am forever grateful to it. I light a candle for it every night, and send off a prayer, and I thank it for allowing the queen conch to find its way to me. It is probably the most perfect present that I have ever been given in my entire life. Thank you, you most precious snail. May you find peace in the sea of eternal life.

"On the night that Robert died...wait. What? YES, he's dead--*that's* not what's important here--let me finish my story. Quit *rudely* interrupting me, darn it! *On the night that Robert died*, I was sitting up in bed holding my shell. It was whispering in my ear of how it felt to feel the ocean floor beneath it. It was telling me that it absolutely loved to see the fish swim above it and around the coral heads. It said that it missed the hum of the motorboats high above. Between its sobs...huh? Yes, shells *do* cry! How *dare* you ask such an insensitive thing? *Ugh! Will you stop talking!* Yes, my queen conch *cries* and *said* that it missed the muffled sounds of voices on an anchored boat, laughing, and it missed the splash that was heard when a person jumped into the water. My queen conch missed all of these things desperately. Though my shell loved me dearly, it missed its home. And, I couldn't blame it. Who could? Could you? We all long for something, don't we?

"That night...the night that Robert died...Robert heard me talking and sat up in bed. He looked at me and told me to shut up, Katia, go back to sleep, Katia, and that he had to work in the morning, Katia. And then he proceeded with his usual diatribe about how *some* of us had to work to pay the bills, and that *some* of us didn't appreciate anything that *he* does, and, what the *hell* was the matter with me. What the hell's the matter with me? How dare he? What the hell's the matter with *him*? What a tone he had! He mumbled some incoherent words under his breath, and to tell you the truth, I think that Robert was swearing at me. SWEARING! The *nerve* of that man...and then he fell back to snoring...

"My shell told me that now was the time. It told me what I had to do...and so I did...I drove the point of the shell deep into Robert's temple. And do you know what? He barely made a sound! Oh, the skin at his temple kind of made a popping, sucking sound. You know, kind of like a mix between the top of a jelly jar being opened up for the first time, and trying to pull your boot out of thick, heavy mud, something like that-- kinda neat--and his blood soiled my nice sheets--dirty bastard--but, Robert, Robert *himself*, left this world very quietly. Can you believe it? The mouthy man that he was all of his life--died graciously. And thankfully, *finally*, his dreadful snoring stopped, which, by the way, allowed me to sleep soundly for the first time in ten years of our marriage. Did you know that he was even gracious enough not to let his blood and urine leak its way to my side of the bed? He even made sure the shit that escaped out of him stayed in his pajama bottoms! I have to admit--that was quite nice of him. I guess I can't deny the fact that he did have *some* manners, after all. Why are you looking at me like that? Quit looking at me like that...stop...stop it...*I said stop it*...

"Yes, I love my queen conch. I love it so much so...it hurts. I miss it so. And, all I have is this picture of it. The real one is evidence now. Sorry, I don't mean to get emotional again, give me a second, okay. I put this picture on the nightstand next to my bed, here. Next to my plastic cup of water and my eyeglasses, here, right here. It is the last thing I see every night before I fall asleep.

"This picture is all that I'm allowed to have in this place. I know! Can you imagine? The *nerve* of these people! Isn't that terrible? I hold the photo to my ear and listen for the whisper. It is distant...but I can still hear my queen conch. And, I know that it's sad. And, I know that it misses me. But I can't do anything about it, so this picture is all that I've got. Usually, though, I have to be quick about holding it this way, next to my ear like this, because, if I'm caught, it's straight to the straitjacket, Katia. Ha ha ha! Funny, huh? That's what they tell me--straight to the straitjacket, Katia. Get it? You get it, right?

"Oh, c'mon, now, that's funny, where is your sense of humor? My best friend. My queen conch. Oh how I love you...you sweet, sweet thing...I like my shell.   My   shell   is   very   pretty."

My Reader,

I do hope that you enjoyed *Normal Collection*.
I'm sure that you did.

In fact--I *know* that you did--you loved it!
(Admit it.)

And--I'm *positive* that you now realize that
Normal Collection really isn't all that normal. It's
abnormal.

And, it's good.

So, please, tell your family and friends about me.
Brag about my work.

Give *Normal Collection* the good feedback that I
know it deserves. I worked hard on it. I spent years
writing these short stories and poems. And, while
you're at it, give all of my books, my precious
brainchildren--my babies--the credit that they
deserve.

Please, do this for me.
Do it NOW!
I will be obeyed. YOU will obey me.
(Sorry--ahem--gotta little carried away there.)

Honestly, word of mouth is *very* important to the
writer. Many do not believe that what we do is hard

work. Many believe that what we write about--anybody can do. But, that is simply not true. Sure, there are times when the words *do* come forth out of our brains and spill out onto the page, but there are those other times, those terrifying (but not in a good way) moments in time, when we struggle and push ourselves to write just one word.

Writer's block is a real thing--and it sucks.

Just so you know, without readers going out there and spreading the word of our talents, we writers will surely perish. We will shrivel up and *die*. This is true. I cannot lie to you. Readers are important to us. Important to *me*.

Without faithful readers like you, we writers will die agonizing, painful deaths--that will last for eternity. You don't want that on your conscious, now, do you? I know that I wouldn't.

So, once again, please, please, tell everyone you know that *Normal Collection* is a fantastic read. It is always important to tell the truth. My life as a writer depends upon your help and compassion.

And, always remember, to read, read everyday. It keeps the mind sharp and the soul young--and ripe for the taking.

Until next time,

J.H.

Born and raised in the state of New York, J.H. now lives in Massachusetts, with her husband and son.

J.H. is the author of ***Brothers Huxten*** and ***Life's Traveled Roads: A Poetry Chapbook.***